LEROY AND THE CAVEMAN

JOEL MATUS

ATHENEUM 1993 NEW YORK

MAXWELL MACMILLAN CANADA
TORONTO

MAXWELL MACMILLAN INTERNATIONAL
NEW YORK OXFORD SINGAPORE SYDNEY

ACKNOWLEDGMENTS

I wish to express thanks to the library staff at the Donald Douglas Museum and Library (now the Museum of Flight) in Santa Monica, California.

Atheneum
Macmillan Publishing Company
866 Third Avenue
New York, NY 10022

Maxwell Macmillan Canada, Inc.
1200 Eglinton Avenue East
Suite 200
Don Mills, Ontario M3C 3N1

Macmillan Publishing Company is part of the
Maxwell Communication Group of Companies.

First edition

Printed in the United States of America

10 9 8 7 6 5 4 3 2 1

The text of this book is set in 12 pt. Palatino.

Book design by Sarah Gonzalez Lauck

LIBRARY OF CONGRESS CATALOGING-IN-PUBLICATION DATA

Matus, Joel.
Leroy and the caveman / Joel Matus.—1st ed.
p. cm.
Summary: In 1942, having been driven by bullies into Dead Man's Canyon, sixth-grader Leroy discovers a living Neanderthal man and is entangled in an adventure involving German spies.
ISBN 0–689–31812–X
1. World War, 1939–1945—United States—Juvenile fiction.
[1. World War, 1939–1945—United States—Fiction. 2. Man, Prehistoric—Fiction. 3. Bullies—Fiction. 4. Spies—Fiction.]
I. Title.
PZ7.M4367Le 1993
[Fic]—dc20 92–24647

For my wife,

Sue,

with love

CONTENTS

PROLOGUE

8:00 P.M., October 5, 1942: A small, green car sped down the coast road that ran by the city of Santa Monica, California.

The driver of the car was a short, plump, white-haired man who looked like a college professor.

His passenger, who was nearly invisible in the dark, sat hunched against the door.

"Just our luck," grumbled the driver. "Not only is it starting to rain, but we enter a dim-out zone at the same time. Not a light on anywhere. The whole city is blacked out!" He nodded his head toward his passenger. "I know, I know. A Japanese sub could see our ships silhouetted against a city's lights. But how are we supposed to see where we're going with just parking lights on?"

He aimed his car in what he hoped was a straight line, clicked off his headlights, and turned on the windshield wipers.

"We can't be late," he continued. "This is important for us."

The driver pushed his glasses closer to his eyes, leaned forward, and wiped the fogged windshield with his hand.

"Damn Hitler and damn General Tojo!" he cursed. "I can't see a thing now."

He flicked on the car's headlights and saw that he was headed toward the curb. "Damn!" he said again and twisted the steering wheel sharply to his left. At the same time, he put his foot down on the brake to slow his speed.

The road was slick, and the small car began to slide.

"Oh!" he exclaimed and jammed his foot back on the gas pedal.

The rear wheels spun wildly, and the back end of the car began to slip around.

"We're going to spin!" he cried, and in a panic he brought his foot down on the brake pedal as hard as he could.

The little car spun like a top. It struck the curb sideways, flipped, and rolled over several times before coming to rest upside down on the sandy beach.

The driver, who had been thrown against the steering wheel and then the roof, lay unconscious in the wrecked car.

The passenger, lying face down on the sand, was also unconscious. His door had sprung open, and he had been hit on the top of the head by it as he was thrown from the car.

The cold rain soon revived him. He pushed himself up into a sitting position, his back to the car. For several minutes he sat with his head in his hands. When he looked up, his eyes were dark and questioning.

Facing him on his right were the bluffs the town was built on. To his left was the entrance to a heavily wooded canyon.

His eyes fixed upon the entrance to the canyon, and he rose to his feet. Standing upright, he was six feet four inches tall.

The part of his face that could be seen through his thick hair and beard had a slightly exaggerated look. His heavily muscled arms were bare, but his thick, powerful body was covered in animal skin down to his knees. Crude fur boots were wrapped around his feet and ankles.

Lying on the sand in front of him were two objects. One was a large club with a stone that had been fitted into the end. The other was a white skull.

The passenger reached down and picked them up. Then he moved quickly across the roadway and disappeared into the dense growth of the canyon.

An hour later, the rain stopped. The little car still lay on its crumpled roof. Inside the car, the driver groaned, but did not open his eyes.

1

NOTHING BUT TROUBLE

"Die, Yankee swine!"

He came racing toward me, an evil gleam in his eyes. His arms were held outward like the wings of the plane he was supposed to be flying. His thumbs, sticking out from his hands were deadly machine guns.

Luckily, I had seen him coming. Spreading my own wings, I took off and headed across the large, grassy, schoolyard field.

"You'll never get me, Nazi dog!"

Another game of fighter-plane tag was on. It was October of 1942, and the United States had been in World War II for ten months.

I looked back. The German Ace, otherwise known

as Charlie Wright, was gaining on me. If he touched me on the shoulder, I was shot down.

A group of boys stood to my left. I decided to go around them. Just as I did, a hand reached out, grabbed my arm, and jerked me off my feet.

"*Ow!*" I hollered.

The grip on my arm tightened.

"Is this the little goon who lost the baseball game for you?" a raspy voice hollered in my ear.

"Hey, let go of me!" I said and tried to pull away.

"Not so fast, *goon!*"

I looked up into the dull, blue eyes of Nick Jordan. Nick was an eighth-grader who had barely gotten through addition and subtraction. He had muscles and he loved to show them off. His fingers dug into my shoulder.

"Ow! Let me go!"

"Give up, twerp!" he said.

"Why don't you go back to the junior high area where you belong."

"Give!" he repeated and squeezed harder.

I gave and stood there looking up at him.

"That's the little goon!" came a voice from behind me. "That's Leroy Penny. He always loses games for us. Don't you, Little Stinkroy?"

I blinked once, hoping that Danny Davis would disappear.

"Cat got your tongue, stupid?" said Danny with a sneer. "You struck out three times today. Albert's team beat us 'cause of you!"

"I got a good idea," said Nick. "Let's fold him like a jackknife and dump him butt first in one of the big trash cans by the lunch benches." With that, he grabbed me around the chest, lifted me up, and began walking.

The benches were up against the main building. Charlie stood forlorn on the sidelines. Several of the prettier girls in my sixth-grade class were sitting there eating and talking. This was going to be a major embarrassment!

I looked for a teacher. None were around, but I was desperate.

"You better let me go!" I said. "Here comes Mrs. Hudson. You're in trouble now. Let me go!" I twisted violently.

Nick hesitated.

"He's lying!" said Danny. "Nobody's around. Come on, Nick, let's dump him."

"A liar, huh?" said Nick. He gave me a shake like a rag doll, and continued moving toward the benches.

All I could see were black-haired Lila, brown-haired Carol, and blond Marie. They would see me dropped in the trash can. They would all laugh at me, and, to make matters worse, tell all the other girls in class what had happened.

Then I had an idea. I would turn a defeat into a victory. As we neared the girls and the trash cans, I smiled up at Nick and said loudly, "All right, slave, take me to my submarine and set me inside!"

"Huh?" said Nick and looked down at me.

"Shut up, Leroy!" said Danny.

"Continue, slave!" I said loudly, my eyes on the three girls.

I thought that everyone would be staring at me as I was dropped into the trash can. Instead, they were all looking up at the sky. Lots of people had started running from the benches out onto the schoolyard.

Nick let go of me and looked at Danny.

"Run!" cried Danny. "Bombers!"

"Come on!" said Nick. They ran to join the others, leaving me to stand alone.

"Look!" shouted a girl who had just run out onto the asphalt. She pointed back toward the rooftop of the main building.

The roar of airplane engines shook the ground and rattled the windows in the building.

I ran in her direction, looking back over my shoulder.

Roaring over the building, only a few hundred feet off the ground, were three twin-engine Douglas Havoc bombers. They were so low that I could see the pilot in the cockpit and the bombardier in the clear nose section of one plane.

"Hey," said someone near me, "the bomb bay doors are open!"

Suddenly the air was filled with hundreds of pieces of paper which fell from the open bomb bays. Caught in the breeze and blown by the propellers, the papers drifted down on the school and the surrounding neighborhood.

"Gimme that!" yelled a boy who ran toward one of the first papers to come down.

"It's mine, *mine!*" hollered another boy. They grabbed the paper at the same moment, ripped it in half, and then started slugging each other.

Everyone wanted a paper. The other students yelled, jumped, shoved, and banged into each other trying to get their hands on one.

I knew I wasn't tall enough to outjump anyone, so I looked for a person who had one.

Not far away from me was a group in a huddle. I ran for them.

"What is it?" I asked.

"A bomb warning," said a seventh-grade boy. "It says that this could have been a Japanese attack. Every house should have bottled water, a bucket of sand to put out fire from incendiary bombs, and blackout curtains so no lights are visible at night."

"Oh, phoo!" said a girl next to me. "This couldn't be a real attack. We've got antiaircraft guns and barrage balloons to protect us."

"So what do you know?" challenged a boy.

"I know what Mrs. Walker told us in class the week they put the barrage balloons up," the girl shot back. "She told us that the steel cables that hold them in place will tear off the wings of any enemy plane that comes in low. They make planes fly up high where our antiaircraft guns can shoot them down."

"Sure," said the boy, "but you don't see any of those little blimps in this neighborhood, do you? That stuff's all around Douglas Aircraft. Planes can come in here as low as they want. I heard on the radio the other night that a Japanese plane dropped a bomb in Oregon. The plane was catapulted off a submarine."

"I heard about that," said another boy. "My dad says we could get bombed anytime."

"Mine too!" said someone else.

"That proves it!" said the first boy. "If one of them bombed Oregon, they could get us too!"

The bell rang, but most of the students stayed in little groups looking at the leaflets.

The planes had brought all the teachers out on the yard. They walked among us saying, "All right, let's get back to class. Lunchtime is over."

As I began walking toward Mrs. Hudson's sixth-grade classroom, a hand clamped down on my shoulder.

"Say, Stinkroy," came Nick Jordan's voice. "I bet you thought those bombers saved you. Well they didn't. We'll see you after school!" As he let go of my shoulder, he gave me a push backward.

"Attaway, Nick," encouraged Danny who stood behind him.

"Let's go to class, boys," said a teacher who walked past us.

Having a teacher near made me braver than I really was. I looked at Danny and blurted out, "Your mother's a hoarder!"

Danny's face became instantly red. "What? Who says?"

"Everybody. Everyone in school knows your mother's got a grocery store full of canned goods in your basement. President Roosevelt said on the radio that hoarding during wartime causes food shortages and it's un-American. So you know what that makes you!"

"Wait a minute," said Danny, a puzzled look on his face. "We don't have a basement. You're a liar!"

"Maybe I was at first, and maybe you don't have a basement. But the way you acted just now tells me the hoarding part is true!"

"You don't know anything, so you better not spread that around!"

"Maybe I will, and maybe I won't."

Another teacher hollered, "Everyone to class!"

"After school," snarled Danny, "you just wait until after school."

He turned, and with Nick began walking to the classrooms.

The courage went out of me like air from a popped balloon. Why had I opened my big mouth? I was really in for it now!

I took a deep breath and with a feeling of doom in my heart, I headed toward my own room.

The first thing we did was to have our weekly spelling test. I carefully wrote my name in the left hand corner of the paper. Under my name went the date, October 6, 1942, and under the date went Mrs. Hudson's name followed by Grade 6, Room 12.

That was about all I got right on the spelling test.

All I could think of was what was going to happen to me after school.

During art session, I tried drawing my favorite comic strip character, a Neanderthal caveman. I knew how to do it by heart, but today it looked more like Donald Duck! During afternoon recess, I went to the rest room and then went right back to the classroom. During silent reading, I could barely concentrate on my story, *Yankee Flyer in the Pacific.*

The sound of the final bell went through me like an electric shock.

Mrs. Hudson, who had been correcting papers, looked up and said, "Class dismissed."

I collected my things and looked toward the doorway. I watched the people pack together and push their way out. Everyone was eager to leave but me.

"Uh . . . Mrs. Hudson?"

"Yes, Leroy?"

"I was wondering if there was anything I could do to help you?"

She looked around the room. "No, Leroy, I don't think so. Thank you for offering, though."

I shifted from one foot to the other. "You're welcome. I'd be glad to stay and help anytime."

"I appreciate that. You run along now. I'll see you tomorrow."

"Okay, bye."

I walked toward the doorway and looked out. The corridor was empty! I went down it quickly and headed across the asphalt toward the gate. That's when I saw them.

They were leaning against the chain-link fence that bounded the tennis courts. They must have run down there as soon as the bell rang.

Nick stepped out and blocked my way. "Why are you walking so fast, Stinkroy? There's no air raid now!"

2

BULLSLINGER

Danny Davis curled his lip and said, "Trying to run home to mama, huh?"

"No," I replied, "my mom's not home. She's running my dad's business while he's in the army."

"Your dad's not really in the army," said Danny.

"He is so!"

"He's not fighting the Japanese or the Germans, is he?"

"No."

"So then he's not really in the army."

"We've got a flag with a star in the window," I said defensively. "You can only have one of those if someone's in the service."

Nick looked at Danny. "What's the deal?"

"His dad's a dancing teacher," said Danny scornfully. "My little sister took tap dancing from him. All his dad does now is put on dancing shows for the army. My mom read an article about it in the newspaper. He's in something called Special Services. They don't fight or nothing!"

"So what's your dad doing that's so great?" I said.

Danny moved closer to me. "Our dads work for Douglas," he said. "They're making bombers. That's a lot more important than tap dancing!"

"Right!" said Nick. He reached for my arm. "Let's dump the little goon!"

I backed away. "I didn't do anything to you, Nick. Why don't you leave me alone?"

Nick stepped forward and stuck his finger in my chest. "I don't like you 'cause of the way you look. How about that?"

Before I could reply, Peanuts McGruder and Marty Ross came by. Although he was small, Peanuts was one of the most feared fighters in school. Marty was his obedient shadow. Both were in seventh grade.

"What's going on here?" asked Peanuts as he clenched and unclenched his fists.

Everyone took a step back.

Danny pointed at me. "Little Leroy here strikes out on purpose every time we play baseball. Nick and I are going to teach him a lesson."

Peanuts looked me up and down. "Is that true?" His fists were clenched.

I shook my head. "No, I don't do it on purpose."

Peanuts nodded and looked at Danny. "Nobody strikes out on purpose."

The sneer on Danny's face disappeared. "Every time we play and he's on our team, we lose because of him. He always strikes out with people still on base."

"So you're no good at baseball," said Peanuts staring hard at me. "What are you good at?"

"He can draw okay," said Marty who was known as one of the best artists in the school. "He does cavemen pretty good."

"I don't like cavemen," said Peanuts and kept staring at me.

I felt desperate. "I can make up stories," I said.

"What kind of stories?" asked Peanuts.

"Come on, Peanuts," said Danny, "leave Nick and me alone with this guy."

"Not so fast. I want to know about the stories."

"I can make up war stories," I said thinking of the book I had been reading. "I can make up a story about how you beat the Japanese in the Pacific."

A slight smile came on Peanuts's lips. "Go ahead."

My mind raced. "You're flying a navy Wildcat over an island in the Pacific. Suddenly, you're jumped by fifteen Japanese Zeros. You shoot down ten of them, but one damages your rudder control, and you have to bail out."

"This sounds interesting," said Peanuts, unclenching his fists. "Go on."

"Your plane spins out of control and crashes in the jungle below. When you parachute down, you see that one of the wings of your plane is blown open. The fifty-caliber machine gun is lying there. You pick it up and wrap a long belt of bullets over your shoulder. Then you start off through the jungle."

"I can't believe this!" exclaimed Danny. "This is stupid. We came down here to—"

"Shut up!" commanded Peanuts. He pointed in my direction. "This guy knows me. That's just what I'd do." He motioned to me. "Go on."

"There are Japanese snipers everywhere," I said dramatically. "They're tied to the tops of palm trees, they're hidden behind fallen logs, they're lying on the roadways pretending to be dead when they're not."

"Great!" exclaimed Peanuts. "What do I do about it?"

"You spray the tops of palm trees with bullets and Japanese soldiers drop like coconuts. When they jump up from behind logs, you mow them down and take their hand grenades.

"Finally you come to a hill overlooking their base."

Danny leaned forward. "Peanuts, I gotta tell you—"

"Butt out, Danny!" Peanuts said threateningly.

Danny looked at Nick for support, but Nick was staring at me, his mouth partly open.

I finished the story. "You spot their ammunition and gasoline. You take out your hand grenades and start tossing! The ammo goes up and so does the whole camp. You get the Congressional Medal of Honor from President Roosevelt!"

Peanuts was nodding. "You got it right. That's just the way it would happen!"

"Say," said Nick. "That was good. Tomorrow, you tell one with me in it, okay?"

"Sure," I replied.

"Wait a minute," demanded Danny, his face as red as a lobster. "We were gonna fry this jerk's butt!"

"He's not such a jerk," said Peanuts.

"No," agreed Marty. "He's not a jerk. He's a . . . he's a bullslinger."

Peanuts laughed. "That's a good one, Marty. We'll call him Bullslinger. See you tomorrow, Bullslinger."

"Sure," I said and began backing away. I wasn't quite sure what Bullslinger meant, but anything that got me out of there was all right with me.

"Hey!" protested Danny angrily.

"Leave Bullslinger alone!" commanded Peanuts.

Danny leaned against the fence and stared angrily at me as I took a few backward steps down the walk. Then I turned and headed for the gate and freedom!

I hadn't gone a block when I knew I was being followed. I spun around and caught a glimpse of someone darting behind a hedge near the alley. It could only be Danny!

I began to walk slowly backward. I decided that when I got to the corner, I'd turn and run for my block. With any luck, I'd make Doc's house on the corner. I would be safe there.

I had taken about a dozen steps when a police car came up the street and pulled over to the curb just in front of me.

"Hello there, Leroy! Is this a new way of watching out for spies, or are you just practicing walking backwards?"

"Hello, Chief," I said and walked across the parkway to the black and white car. "I'm just practicing walking backwards, I guess."

"Then that fellow crouching down behind the hedge back there doesn't have anything to do with you?"

"No, I don't think so." I lied.

Police Chief Charles West was a family friend. He and my dad grew up together. We hadn't seen much of him, though, since the United States entered the war.

"How are you and your mother getting along without your dad?" he asked.

"I miss him, but he writes a lot. He just sent me some army shoulder patches."

The chief nodded. "It was very patriotic of your father to volunteer like he did. You tell your mom that I'll drop by this evening, say hello, and get your dad's new address."

"Okay, I will."

He put the car in gear, started to pull away from

the curb, and then stopped. I could tell he was looking in his rearview mirror.

I looked at the spot where Danny had been hiding. For a second I didn't see him. Then I did. He had left the hedge and had walked out onto the parkway. He was standing under a tree, hands in pockets, staring in my direction.

"Leroy," called the chief. "I'm going your way. Would you like a lift?"

"Yes, thanks, Chief. I would." I opened the door, stepped up on the running board, and got inside.

The chief glanced at me as he pulled away from the curb. "I had a lot of differences with boys I knew when I was your age. As I remember, most problems tended to blow over by the next day if you gave them a chance."

"I don't know about Danny, but I'll give it a chance."

"Good. You do that and the problem might solve itself."

"Yes, sir."

We quickly drove the block and a half to my street. I got out and closed the door.

"Thanks, Chief. I'll tell my mom that you'll call."

He nodded. "You take care, now," he said, and drove off.

I looked across the street and saw Doc pruning a bush in his backyard. He was a retired dentist and lived in the house with his granddaughter Melissa.

"Hi, Doc!" I called.

"Hello, Leroy," he called back. "That's a pretty fancy ride home you got for yourself."

"The chief wanted to know about my dad," I said as I crossed the street. As I did, I gave a quick look down the block but saw no sign of Danny.

"Did you see the bombers?" I asked as I opened the gate and entered the yard.

"Yes, I did," he replied. "Speaking of the bombers, Melissa has something for you."

The back door slammed, and Melissa came down the steps. "Hi, Leroy. Wasn't that something when the airplanes flew over school today?"

I looked in her hand and saw that she held one of the leaflets. "How did you get that?" I asked in amazement. "The other kids were fighting for them."

She laughed. "This one came down in Doc's yard, and he got it. You can have it. We've got lots because Doc's the Air Raid Warden for our block. He's got an envelope full to give to people who didn't get one."

"Thanks," I said and carefully slid the paper into my math book.

Melissa's parents had been killed in a plane crash, which was why she was living with Doc. She was smart, and she was pretty. I liked her, but I didn't have much to do with her at school. I didn't want guys hollering, "Leroy's got a girlfriend!"

"Want to ride bikes to the drugstore?" she asked.

"Now, Melissa," said Doc, "you haven't had your

rest yet. You don't want to end up like poor Willie Owens, do you?"

A look passed across Melissa's face that meant she wanted to answer back, but she didn't. Doc hardly ever let her out of his sight, even before Willie got polio. Now he was worse.

"All of you youngsters should get extra rest after school," Doc said. "Being rested is one of the best safeguards against getting polio."

"I heard that Willie got home on Monday, but I haven't seen him," I said.

"No," said Doc, "he hasn't been out yet. But I talked to Mrs. Owens, and he will be soon. Well . . . you better go home and wait for your mother."

"Okay, bye, Doc; see you, Melissa," I said and walked to the gate.

"Oh, Leroy," said Doc. "Be sure to tell your mother to read the article in this evening's paper about the spies."

I turned. "What spies? Are there spies here?"

"There might be," he said. "One of the captured Germans who landed back east has been talking to the FBI. It looks like some dangerous saboteurs may be on their way to California. Don't forget now. I know your mother's tired when she gets home from work, but everyone should know about it. We can't be too careful these days."

As I closed the gate behind me, I looked back down the street toward school. There were lots of bushes and hedges where someone could hide and wait.

I was so intent on looking behind me, that I didn't pay any attention to the hedge in front of Doc's house.

With a sigh of relief, I rounded the corner . . . and walked straight into Danny Davis!

3

OF POLIO AND SPIES

"Police protection, huh?" said Danny and reached out and gave my shoulder a shove.

"Let me alone."

"Why should I, Bullslinger? Tell me why I should leave you alone?"

"I didn't do anything to you."

"Yes you did. You called my mother a hoarder, and you make our team lose baseball games at school."

"I didn't ask to be on your team."

"No, but you're almost always the last one chosen, and most of the time we get you. You've never gotten one hit when you play for us. I think you do it on purpose."

"That's a lie!"

"So's what you said about my mother being a hoarder. Nobody calls my mother names and gets away with it!"

"I'm going home," I said, and made a quick move to my right. I got around him and took a dozen steps down the street before he managed to block my path again.

"Get out of my way, Danny."

"Why should I? Look around, Leroy, there's nobody to protect you now, is there?"

"Yes there is."

He laughed. "Who? I don't see anybody. No police cars and no mommy to protect her baby!"

He took a step toward me, and I backed away.

"What's the matter, Bullslinger? Come on, I'll even let you hit me first. Here, hit my shoulder hard as you want!" He turned his left shoulder toward me and sneered.

"I'm not going to touch you," I replied. "I don't have to."

"Oh, yeah?" he said and straightened up. "Just tell me why not. 'Cause you're gonna get it whether you tell me or not."

"Because," I said slowly, "Peanuts said to leave me alone. You heard him. He expects me to tell another story tomorrow. If you mess with me now, I'm going to tell him at recess."

"Yeah?"

"Yeah, for sure. Touch me and you'll have to fight Peanuts!"

An uncertain look came into Danny's eyes. I could tell that he was trying to figure out how much truth there was in what I'd said. Suddenly, he slumped and stuffed his hands deeply into his pockets.

"All right," he said, "so tell your story tomorrow. In a few days, Peanuts will get tired of your dumb stories and will forget all about you. I'll get you then!" He gave me a wounded sneer and headed up the block.

My legs felt rubbery. I walked over to the curb and sat down.

Lying against the curb was a large leaf. I picked it up by the stem. It was brown and hard. I sat there, twirling it in my fingers and staring at the street.

"Hi, Leroy!"

The call came from across the street. I looked up and saw Willie Owens sitting in a wheelchair a couple of houses down. His mother stood behind him. She must have just pushed him out from the backyard. I'd heard that they had built a ramp down their back stairs. Mrs. Owens waved at me and then went up the front steps and into the house.

"Hey," called Willie, "have you seen Douglas Aircraft? My dad took me yesterday. Why don't you come over?"

"Sure," I called back. I let go of the leaf and got to my feet.

I walked slowly across the street and stopped about six feet from him. It felt funny to be looking down at him.

"So," he said looking up at me through round, horn-rimmed glasses, "you haven't seen Douglas?"

"No," I replied. "Some guys at school said that it was being camouflaged to look like a hill with houses on it."

"Right," he said. "My dad worked on it. The engineers stretched a chicken-wire net from the ground over the tops of all the buildings. Then they put fiberglass over the net and painted it to look like a hill with streets. The houses are nothing but burlap and chicken wire, but they look real from far away. They even put fake bushes and trees on it."

While he was talking, I was looking him over. He was a bit thinner, otherwise he looked the same. His blond hair still stuck out in all directions. His voice and manner were the same. Nothing about him was really different except for the wheelchair.

"So," he said squinting up at me, "you made any model airplanes lately?"

"Yeah, I just finished a solid model of a fighter called the Brewster Buffalo. It took me a week to carve out the body and sand it right. You got any new stamps?"

He nodded. "My uncle brought me a lot of stamps when I was in the hospital. And here, look at this." He fished in his side pocket and then extended his hand.

I took the small copper coin and looked closely at it.

Willie said, "It's an 1880 Indian head penny. You don't see many Indian heads anymore. My uncle said it was his good luck coin. He said if I rubbed it once a day it would help me to walk sooner."

"Then I'd rub it twice a day."

"That's what my doctor said. That's dumb, though. Doctors aren't supposed to be superstitious. I don't think I'll ever walk again. That's okay, though. President Roosevelt had polio, and he can't walk either. That didn't stop him from becoming president."

"I guess not," I said, "but I'd still rub the coin."

"I suppose," he said doubtfully.

Willie's eyes scanned the sky. "Look!" he cried and pointed over my shoulder.

I turned around and looked up. "It's the B-19!"

"That's why I'm out here," he said. "My dad told me they would be testing it this afternoon."

We watched as the giant olive-colored four-engine bomber, half a football field long, flew overhead.

"Wow!" exclaimed Willie. "We're really lucky, you know. How many guys get to see them testing the biggest plane in the world?"

The B-19 was now directly overhead and we were craning our necks to follow it.

"Can you believe," said Willie, "that the tail is four stories high?"

"Yeah," I said, but my eyes were on the two, huge eight-foot balloon tires that were neatly folded under its wings. I had seen a photograph in the paper of a woman standing next to the wheels, dwarfed by their size. It was my dream to get as close to the plane as that woman.

Our eyes followed the B-19 as it flew north over the Santa Monica Mountains and disappeared from sight.

"That was great!" I said.

A breeze kicked up, and some dried leaves clattered along the sidewalk. Willie was silent, looking down at his legs.

"Well," I said, "I've got to do my chores before my mom gets home from work. She counts on me a lot now."

Willie looked up. "Sure, Leroy, it's been nice seeing you. Maybe you can stop by sometime. Just knock on the door and my mom will let you in."

"Okay, Willie. And don't forget to rub that Indian head."

He managed a smile. "Right. And I really mean it about coming over."

"Sure," I replied.

I turned and ran across the street, waved back at him, and continued down to my house.

"Will Captain Harrington fall victim to the sinister Nazi agent, M12? And what will happen to Dawn Patrol members Dave and Jane who are at this moment on their way into a deadly trap set by Colonel Von Shrank? Tune in tomorrow, for the further adventures of . . . Rick Harrington and the Dawn Patrol!"

It was 5:30. I clicked off the radio and heard the soft thud of the evening paper hitting the front steps.

I brought the paper inside, slid off the rubber band, and unfolded it to the headline: WATCH FOR THESE SPIES!

Under the headline were close-up photographs of three men. Their names were Heinz Muller, Ernst Wald, and Werner Bauer. They stared at me with cold, unsmiling faces.

I clicked on the lamp, sat down on the couch and read:

> The FBI has issued wanted circulars in Washington giving the identities of three expert German saboteurs ordered to the United States to destroy vital war industries.
>
> J. Edgar Hoover, director of the FBI, announced that the following information comes from papers taken from a band of Nazi spy-saboteurs who were landed by U-boats on the East Coast and are now in FBI custody.
>
> Hoover stated that the saboteurs will be dressed as civilians and will carry forged social security and draft cards.
>
> "The three men have all lived, worked, and

traveled widely in the United States before the war," he said. "They speak perfect English. They were brought back to Germany in 1939 and trained as master saboteurs by the Nazi High Command.

"They will be carrying a large amount of payoff money to be used as bribes. Among weapons already taken from spies like these have been mechanical exploding devices that can be set to go off days later, TNT, bombs disguised as pieces of coal, fire-producing acids, flare pencils, and incendiary pens that give off sheets of flame that will ignite anything."

Santa Monica police chief Charles West said that all civilians should keep a close watch for enemy agents who may attempt to land on the Southern California coast.

"Evidence such as abandoned rubber boats, abandoned clothing, or anything pointing to suspicious landings should be reported at once," he stated.

I folded the paper and set it down on the couch. The faces of the three spies stared up at me. I wondered where they were and what they were doing at this moment.

The house was still. From one of the back rooms

came the creak of a floorboard. Drops of water from a leaky faucet on the back porch made hollow tapping sounds as they fell into the basin.

It was creepy being in the house all alone. I got up and walked over to a nearby table. Picking up my schoolbooks, I turned on the porch light, and headed out the front door. I spent the next hour on the bottom step doing my homework.

Every once in a while I would look through the window at the clock that sat on the mantelpiece. At 6:45, I walked toward the front of the yard and sat down on the curb. From there I could see to the end of the block.

Ten minutes later, my mother's car rounded the corner, and I stood and waved.

At seven o'clock that evening, the doorbell rang.

"Leroy," called my mother from the kitchen. "See who's there, will you?"

I opened the door to Chief West.

"Hello, Leroy, is your mother home?"

"Sure," I replied, and let the chief in.

He talked with my mother for a while, got my father's army address, and then turned to me. "We've had a little incident down at the beach that I think will interest you, Leroy."

I was puzzled. "At the beach?"

"Yes," he said. "We found a wreck. It looks as though it happened around eight o'clock yesterday evening. An elderly man was driving south on the coast road. He was probably speeding, and the road was wet. Looks like he lost control of his car. It skidded, hit the curb, and rolled over onto the beach. No one seems to have seen the accident. It wasn't reported until the coast watch was changed and the new team came on."

"Was the man killed?" asked my mother.

"No," replied the chief. "He was lucky. Nothing was broken. He did get a nasty bump on the head though. The doctors say he has a concussion. Now here's the interesting part. He's unconscious, but every so often, he talks a bit."

"What does he say?" I asked.

"Well," said the chief, "that's why I'm telling you the story. I know how interested you are in cavemen. And that's what he talks about. He keeps mumbling about being late for something, then he says, 'Energy field experiment . . . surprise . . . Neanderthal man!' "

I shook my head. "That doesn't make sense. The Neanderthals lived over forty thousand years ago."

"Did the man have any identification?" asked my mother.

"His driver's license is from Nebraska. His name is Robert Ludlow. One of my officers looked in the trunk of his car and found a very strange-looking electrical contraption. It's made up of a lot of coiled copper wire and copper tubing. The officers at the station have bets on what it will turn out to be."

"What do they think it is?" I asked.

"Everything," laughed the chief, "from a coffee percolator to a time machine."

"Good heavens!" exclaimed my mother. "Why a time machine?"

"Well," said the chief, "first there were Mr. Ludlow's mumblings, then there were a couple of other things we found in the trunk. There was a framed college diploma from the University of London naming Robert Ludlow a professor of electrical engineering. Then there were two suitcases of clothing. One case held clothes that were Mr. Ludlow's size. The other case held clothes that belonged to a big man with a very large neck and chest size. Oh, and there was a pair of broken handcuffs lying on the sand near the car. We don't know whether they came from the car or not. At any rate, all of that set some imaginations going."

I got excited. "Supposing that it is a time machine! Supposing there is a Neanderthal man! What would you do if you found him?"

The chief let out a loud, deep laugh. "Well, I don't know, Leroy. I don't think I've taken that thought seriously. If he was uncontrollable, say like a bull in a china shop, I suppose we might have to shoot him."

"But Chief!" I protested.

He stood and laughed again. "Leroy, I wouldn't worry about anything like that happening. I'm quite sure that there is no Neanderthal. The doctors think the old fellow will come out of this in a few days.

When he does, we'll probably find a reasonable explanation for his mumblings." He looked down at me and smiled. "Now this is sort of a military secret. At least until we can find out where he was going in such a hurry. I can count on you to keep quiet about it, can't I?"

"Sure, Chief," I replied. "But if there is a Neanderthal, promise you won't hurt him."

"Leroy," said the chief laughing. "You're worse than some of the men at the station!" He turned to my mother. "Good night, Mrs. Penny. Good night, Leroy."

My mother held the door for him, and we heard him laughing to himself all the way out to his car.

At 8:30 that evening, I was lying on my bed looking at the shoulder patches I'd received from my dad the day before.

"Hi," said my mother poking her head in my open doorway.

"Come in," I said.

She walked into the room and sat on the corner of the bed. "I see you've got the front page of the paper. I was wondering where it went."

The paper sat near my pillow, folded so the faces of the spies were visible.

"Sorry, I forgot I had it."

"Are you memorizing them?"

"I got to thinking about it," I said. "If they are in

Santa Monica, I wouldn't want to walk by one of them and not know it. What if they tried to blow up Douglas?"

She nodded. "When you think you've got them in your mind, I'd like to read the paper."

"Oh, you can have it now." I reached over and handed it to her.

"Lights out in fifteen minutes," she said.

"All right . . . Mom?"

"Yes?"

"Do you get scared sometimes with Dad not being around?"

She moved closer to me and put her hand gently on my shoulder. "I miss him."

"No, I mean with spies around and stuff like those airplanes today, do you get scared we might get bombed?"

"Yes, but I think being scared in wartime is perfectly normal. Do you feel scared sometimes?"

"I guess so, sometimes." I looked on the wall by my bed. All the pictures were of airplanes except one. That was a picture from the back cover of a comic book. It showed a caveman riding on the back of a dinosaur. There was a large club in his hand and a determined look on his face. "I wish the Neanderthal man the chief was talking about was real and could be on our side. He'd really be able to take care of those spies."

My mother laughed. "Yes he would. I'll bet he could take a dozen out with one swing of that club."

"I saw Willie Owens today," I said. "He was sitting out in front of his house. We saw the B-19." I pushed a couple of patches around on my quilt.

"How was Willie?"

"I don't know. He's decided that he's never going to walk again. Do you think that's true?"

"No, I don't. I've talked to his mother. Willie had a mild case of polio, and it was detected quickly. He had some paralysis in his legs, but that's over now. In fact, his doctor feels that he should be walking."

"Then why is he in the wheelchair?"

"The doctor thinks that Willie is afraid that if he tries and fails, it will mean he'll never walk again."

"But that's stupid! If he doesn't try, he never will."

"Polio is a scary thing to get. We haven't been sick like Willie has."

I pushed my patches into a circle. "I was pretty close to him when we were talking. . . ."

My mother looked at me for a moment and then said, "Are you afraid you'll get polio by being near him?"

"Well . . ."

She shook her head. "No, the doctors kept Willie in isolation when he could spread it. He's all right now. I wouldn't be afraid of him. He needs friendship, not fear." She reached over and gave me a hug. Then she took the paper, and started to walk out the door.

"Mom . . ."

She turned. "Yes?"

"What's a bullslinger?"

"It means someone who doesn't tell the truth."

"Like a liar . . . someone who makes up lies?"

"That's right. Did you hear it at school?"

"Yeah," I said, "a couple of guys were talking about a third grader."

"Well," she said, "it wasn't very nice. Good night." She walked down the hallway and into the living room.

My face burned! I got my patches together and stuffed them into the envelope they'd come in. Then I got ready for bed.

Ten minutes later, I lay in the dark, my hands behind my head, staring up at the shadows on the ceiling.

I thought about my dad being gone, and how I wished he was at home. I thought about Danny Davis, and how I wished I could beat him up. And I thought of Marty who'd called me Bullslinger, and who was protected by Peanuts. I thought about the German spies, and I thought about the Neanderthal. I wished he were real, and I wished he were my friend. I'd be able to use his help because I wasn't going to tell stories to people who laughed at me and called me a fancy word for liar!

With these thoughts in mind, I fell asleep.

4

NOT A COWARD

I awoke the next morning with the same feelings I'd had the night before.

I jumped out of bed and walked over to my dresser. I spoke to it as though it were a person—Peanuts McGruder to be exact.

"I am not telling any war stories to people who call me a name like Bullslinger!" I said loudly.

"What, dear?" came my mother's voice from the hall.

"Nothing, Mom," I hollered through the closed door. "Just practicing a poem for class today."

"Want to say it for me? I'd love to hear it."

"No, I don't think so. It will be fine. I'll do it for you later."

I glared at the chest of drawers one final time. "I'm

not a bullslinger!" I said angrily. I gave it a shove. Then, satisfied with my courage, I opened a drawer and got out my clothes.

A half an hour later, I was ready to leave.

"Bye, Mom!"

"Have a good day, Leroy!" came her voice from the bathroom.

I grabbed my books and headed out the back gate. I went up the alley and crossed a vacant lot.

"Morning, Leroy," said Melissa, coming up behind me. "Bet you weren't supposed to go up the alley."

"My mom doesn't care," I said.

"Your mom didn't see, and I won't tell." She smiled.

I smiled. We walked to school together.

"Leroy's got a girlfriend!" greeted us as we turned through the school gate.

I looked over to where the call came from and saw a bunch of guys kneeling down shooting marbles. "Never mind, Melissa, just ignore them," I said with newfound confidence.

We continued to walk toward the lunch-box cabinets that lined the walls outside the rooms. We put our lunches away, walked over to the main building, sat on some benches, and talked until the first bell rang.

At lunchtime, I was met at the classroom door by the German Ace.

"Heil Hitler!" he said snapping his arm out stiff in the Nazi salute. "American Ace vishes to eat lunch before being shot down?"

"Heil your B-hind!" I replied, putting my thumb to my nose and wiggling my fingers. "It will be your last meal!"

"Vee shall zee!" he replied with narrowed eyes.

After we had eaten, we headed out to the crowded playing field to begin our game.

"Take off!" he shouted.

"Take off!" I replied.

He immediately disappeared around a group of younger boys who were playing with yo-yos. I headed after him, but I didn't get very far.

"Hey, Bullslinger!"

I dropped my arms, and looked around.

"Over here, Bullslinger!" called Peanuts. He was standing against a tether-ball pole near the grass. With him were Nick, Marty, and Danny.

"Got you, American dog!" cried the German Ace and slapped me on the shoulder. I was so startled I jumped.

"What's wrong?" Charlie asked.

"I can't play for a while," I said. "See you later."

He lowered his wings and looked a bit hurt. "But that counts, doesn't it?"

"Sure, it counts. I just forgot that I've got to do something." I turned and began walking toward Peanuts.

"We been waiting for you, Bullslinger," said Nick. "Today you tell my story, right?"

I sucked in a deep breath and let it out. "No, I'm not telling any stories to anyone who calls me names."

"Hey," said Peanuts, his hands formed into fists, "who called you a name?"

"You did when you called me a bullslinger."

"That's 'cause we like you," he said and winked at Marty. "Now come on, Bullslinger, tell us that story about Nick and the war."

I shook my head. "Forget it! Bullslinger means a liar, and you can't tell me different!" With that, I turned and walked as quickly as I could toward the ball box.

"Hey, Bullslinger, come back here!" called Nick. "Hey, I want my story you little jerk!"

"Come here!" hollered Peanuts. But I kept walking.

The ball box was a small shed that contained soccer balls, basketballs, softballs, and bats. During lunch it was staffed by a teacher who was in charge of checking out the equipment.

I looked inside and saw that Mrs. Burns, the first-grade teacher, was alone.

"Hi, Mrs. Burns. Would you like some help?"

"Why thank you, Leroy, I certainly would." She opened the bottom part of the door and let me in. This would give me protection for the rest of the lunch period.

Peanuts casually strolled by once and looked in at me. I saw him and pretended to be busy counting baseballs. He stopped, pointed at me, and made a fist. I knew that meant I was in for it after school. I'd have to leave fast and try to get out the front of the school instead of the back as I usually did.

The quickest way out the front was straight up the hallway, but that's where Peanuts's class was. The other way was to cross the yard behind the main building and then go up the corridor between it and the kindergarten. That's what I'd do.

"See you all tomorrow," said Mrs. Hudson as the dismissal bell rang.

I was first out of the door and running. I made it to the kindergarten and headed up the corridor. I dodged around several people. The sidewalk was in view. I was like a football player on an open field. The sidewalk was my goal line. I was almost there—but not quite.

"You were right!" came Nick's voice. "There he goes. Grab him, Peanuts!"

"I got him!" came Peanuts's voice from my right.

I turned to see Peanuts descending upon me and Nick running, red-faced behind him. Danny and Marty were both coming up the corridor behind me. I was caught.

"What's the big idea, say?" huffed Nick. "You

were supposed to tell my story today. What'd you hide in the ball box for?"

"I said I don't like being called a bullslinger."

"That's just tough, ain't it?" snarled Peanuts, his hands curled into fists. "Because a bullslinger is just what you are!"

"I am not! I just told a story, and you liked it."

Peanuts waved his fist in my face. "Yeah, I did like it. It was just what I'd do if I was in the war. So yesterday you were a good bullslinger. But today, you're just a little bullslinger, period! Nobody tells us off and then runs out on us, see?"

Danny Davis stepped up. "I told you he was a little jerk! You didn't believe me before. The way he tried to run away makes him a little coward too."

"I'm no coward!" I replied hotly.

"Says you!" growled Peanuts. "We figured you'd try to escape this way, and that's just what you did. You going to stand there and tell us that this is the way you usually go home from school?"

"Yeah," said Nick, shoving a finger into my ribs. "Answer that one, Bullslinger."

"I'm not a bullslinger, and I'm not a coward either."

"Then prove it, twerp!" said Danny with a sneer. "Prove you're not a coward."

I looked at their faces. Each one was staring at me and waiting for my reply. Yesterday, I'd saved myself with a war story. What could I do today? I closed my eyes tightly and across my mind flashed the words.

"The canyon!" I blurted out.

"What?" said a startled Danny.

"Dead Man's Canyon," I repeated slowly. "I'll prove to you that I'm not a coward. I'll go down into Dead Man's Canyon."

"You're nuts!" exclaimed Nick. "Nobody goes down there. That's where murderers dump bodies."

"That was in the nineteen twenties," I replied.

"What about the hobo murders five years ago?" asked Marty. "Somebody killed four of those guys and chopped them up in little pieces."

I was cool. "That was five years ago. Nothing has happened since then."

"Nothing anyone knows about," said Marty. "That place is so full of trees that you can hardly see into it. And it runs all the way out to the ocean. Anybody could be in it, and anything could go on."

"Besides, there're No Trespassing signs all around it," said Danny. "You won't go down there. You're just bluffing."

"Yeah," said Nick to Peanuts. "He's bluffing. Let's just take him to a vacant lot and beat him up."

"No," answered Peanuts. "Let's take him to the canyon right now and let him show us how brave he is."

"Good idea," agreed Danny, a sneer coming back on his face. "It's just about a mile and a half from here."

"I can't," I said quickly. "I've got to go home and help my mother. She's expecting me, and she'll send out the police if I'm not home! I'll do it tomorrow."

"You really are a bullslinger," said Peanuts. "Get moving or we *will* take you to the vacant lot."

I turned and started to walk slowly up the street. It would take half an hour to get there. Maybe I could think of some way to escape on the way.

Peanuts, who was walking next to me and staring hard into my face, read my mind. "Don't try nothing funny, Bullslinger!"

"I'm not trying anything," I replied.

"Better not," he threatened, "because if you do, I'll throw you down into the canyon headfirst!"

"Let me throw him down headfirst!" said Nick eagerly from behind me.

"Sure," said Peanuts, "why not, Nick. If he tries anything, he's yours."

Peanuts gave me a shove, and we crossed the street. The neighborhood was well-kept and quiet. Not many people were out.

An old lady who was setting a sprinkler on her lawn looked up and said cheerfully, "Hello, boys."

"Good afternoon, ma'am," replied Danny with a large, phony smile.

We walked along in silence. I tried to figure out how I could escape from them, but nothing came. I was still trying to figure something out when we arrived at our destination.

Houses were built right up to the street before the canyon, but none were built on its rim.

There were about fifty yards of field before the canyon's edge. Scattered palm and eucalyptus trees dotted the field. Weeds that were plowed under twice a year filled in between them.

We were almost to the rim when Danny said, "Smell that odor?"

"Yeah," said Peanuts, "it must be the dead bodies."

Marty stared at me and shook his head like someone who was looking at a dead person at a funeral.

For a minute, we all stood and stared down at the canopy of leaves that covered the canyon.

"Let's throw him down headfirst!" said Nick.

A shiver went through me, and I felt the hair on the back of my neck stand up like a cat's.

"All right, Bullslinger," said Peanuts. "You're full of war stories. Show us how brave you really are!"

What could I do? "Sure," I said. "Nothing to it!" And without looking back, I stepped over the rim and started down the steep side.

Danny's voice shot out from behind me, "A new Duncan yo-yo says the baby never makes the bottom."

"Red and black or free-wheeler?" asked Peanuts.

"Free-wheeler with a jewel on the side," replied Danny.

"You're on!" said Peanuts. "And to make sure that the baby does make the bottom, I'm gonna help him along with some hand grenades!"

The next thing I knew, dirt clods were landing near me.

"Get moving, Bullslinger!" cried Peanuts.

"Cut it out!" I hollered back. "I said I'd go down, didn't I?"

"You think I'd believe what a bullslinger says?" hollered Peanuts, and he threw another dirt clod near me.

"No fair!" argued Danny. "We never said you could use dirt clods."

"They're hand grenades," replied Peanuts. "And we never said nothing about not using no hand grenades!"

I grabbed on to the stalks of bushes to keep from losing my footing on the steep descent. Once, I stopped at the smooth, gray trunk of a small eucalyptus that was growing out of the canyon's side.

A dirt clod smashed near my foot.

"Move it!" yelled Peanuts.

I let go of the tree and grabbed at the frond of a large fern as the dirt gave way under my weight.

The canyon wall went down at a forty-five degree angle. There weren't many plants at the top, but the farther down I went, the thicker the growth became.

I picked my way through the skeletonlike branches of a dead tree, slid on my fanny, and grabbed at rocks, branches, and vines for support.

When I reached the bottom, my hands were scratched and burning and my pants were covered with dirt. There was all kinds of junk inside my shoes, so I sat down and started pulling them off.

A dirt clod landed next to me, and I jumped.

"You just cost me a quarter, you little jerk!" hollered Danny, and another clod landed about four feet away from me.

I ran for the cover of a large tree. My mistake was that as I ran, I looked back over my shoulder for falling dirt clods.

I ran right into a giant spider web! "Ahh!"

In fear that a spider was on me, I began beating at my clothes and brushing my hair.

"Catch a bug, Bullslinger?" hollered Danny.

That stopped me. I ducked under the branches and kept my eyes on the business of getting where I wanted to be. When I reached the trunk of the tree, I dropped down on the soft, damp ground.

It was dark and the air was thick and smelly.

A twig was lying nearby. I picked it up and began idly flipping some of the broad leaves that covered the ground. The third one I flipped uncovered the body of a dead bird. I pushed a mass of leaves back over it and moved away to my left.

"Hey, Bullslinger," came Peanuts's voice. "We ain't leaving until the sun goes down. You'll have a tough time getting out of here then. You better get exploring. Maybe you'll find a secret way out."

"Yeah," hollered Danny, "or maybe you'll find another dead body!"

I closed my eyes and tried to pretend that I was sitting on the couch at home. Then I heard a noise, opened my eyes, and saw a large lizard. That did it! I jumped to my feet and went out the back side of the tree.

Keeping low, so that there would be no chance of being seen from the rim, I picked my way between trees and bushes. I headed away from the guys and toward the ocean.

The ground was dappled by drops of sunlight that shifted about as the breeze nudged the trees. I stopped and looked about. Trees loomed overhead now, completely blocking my view of the canyon walls. Limbs spread and dropped. Weeds, ferns, ivy, and bushes all competed for ground space.

Instead of feeling frightened, I found that I felt better. If I couldn't see Peanuts, he couldn't see me! I was on my own and safe from them. I'd go on a little farther, then turn toward the canyon wall, climb out, and go safely home.

Carefully, I picked my way between a pine tree and a giant bush and found myself in a narrow clearing and about twenty feet from a large willow. Its shape reminded me of pictures I had seen of Indian huts.

I became curious and wanted to see what it looked like from inside the branches. I walked across the clearing, pushed the branches aside, stepped in, and came face-to-face with a bleached, white skull!

5

THE NEANDERTHAL

The skull was set on the end of a long stick which had been pushed into the ground. It stared at me with empty eye sockets. I stared back and felt hypnotized. I couldn't take my eyes off of it.

The empty eye sockets seemed to be pulling at me. Slowly, I began to walk toward the skull.

Crack!

From somewhere behind the tree, a branch was broken and then another. Someone was coming!

I took an unsteady step backward onto a rounded stone that was half-buried in the ground. My foot slid, and I sat down hard.

That's when I realized that the skull wasn't human. It belonged to some type of large animal. It had a snout, and the teeth in its jaw were large and sharp.

I looked at the ground below the skull. A small circle of stones had been placed neatly around the base of the stick.

Another branch cracked, and a shuffling sound came from behind the tree. I judged it was from the right side. I was wrong. I turned and bolted straight through the branches on the left side and stopped dead in my tracks.

There, about twenty feet away from me, stood a caveman! He was dressed in a tunic of animal skins. In his hand was a huge club with a rock fitted in the end of it and tied with vines. His mouth was partly open and his teeth, framed by his black beard, looked more like a lion's than a man's.

He was a giant! And if he got his hands on me, he'd kill me and eat me and stick my skull on a stick next to the animal's!

I turned and ran as fast as I could! It was one thing to think about meeting a caveman. It was quite another to come face-to-face with a real one!

I ran without looking back. I didn't have to. I knew that he would be after me.

I ran through bushes I should have gone around. I ran through low branches that poked and scratched and tried to hold me back.

Several times I tripped, but each time I managed to fling my arms about and keep my balance. I ran until I got to the canyon wall where I'd come down.

Please, I thought, as I plunged forward, let them still be there! Please, let them help me when they see me! I've got to have help. Please!

As I burst from the trees I glanced upward at the canyon rim. They were gone!

For a moment, I wasn't sure what to do. If I yelled, he'd hear me. I couldn't stay on the canyon floor. My only chance was to climb the steep side as fast as I could.

Grabbing eagerly at low-hanging branches, I began my race up the canyon wall. Roots like those that had tripped me as I ran were now my allies in escape. I grabbed at them with my hands and pushed at them with my feet.

My arms and legs never stopped moving. Sweat ran into my eyes and blurred my vision. My mouth became dry and tacky. All my muscles ached.

Once, I thought I heard him grunting somewhere below me, and I doubled my efforts.

When I reached the top, I was totally exhausted. Gasping for breath, I pulled myself up over the rim and lay panting on the ground. With great fear, I turned my head and looked down the canyon side. It was empty.

My eyes scanned every inch of the canyon wall and the trees below, but I saw nothing. He wasn't behind me after all!

Gratefully, I put my head on my arm and slobbered a big dark spot on my sleeve.

I couldn't believe what I had seen. A caveman, a real caveman was living in the canyon!

Suddenly, Chief West's visit came back to me. I'd been so scared, I hadn't thought about it. I heard him repeat the words of the unconscious, old man. "Energy field experiment . . . surprise . . . Neanderthal man!"

The old man wasn't just babbling. There *was* a Neanderthal. And the funny-looking electrical contraption might just be a time machine.

After a few minutes, my breath came easier. I got up and ran across the field and toward the safety of sidewalks, houses, and people. I continued in a half-trot until I had put one long block between the canyon and myself.

By the time I reached school, I was beginning to feel more excitement than fear.

I began to wonder about the Neanderthal. Could he speak? If he had been with the professor for long, had he learned any English? Most of all, I began to wonder what would have happened if I hadn't run away. I thought about his eyes. They looked surprised. Was it possible that if I had stayed, he wouldn't have killed me?

Deep in thought, I followed the sidewalk toward my house.

* * *

"Gosh, Leroy, what happened to you?"

I looked up and saw that I was by Melissa's backyard. She walked up to the picket fence and stood waiting for my reply.

"Melissa, I was down in Dead Man's Canyon, and I saw a real Neanderthal man. He's living down there right now!"

"Very funny, Leroy! Nobody goes into that canyon. What happened to you, really?"

"Cross my heart, no lie, this is what really happened." I told her the whole story.

When I finished, she shook her head. "I know you don't lie, but you do have a very strong imagination. First there was that movie *One Million B.C.* You saw cavemen in your dreams after that. Then there were all those books from the library. Now you draw that comic book caveman all the time."

"So what's your point?" I said defensively.

"It's just that for the last year you've had cavemen on your mind nearly all the time. If you were where you say you were, are you sure that you just didn't see some dirty old bum with a beard?"

"Come on, Melissa, this was a real Neanderthal. His head was thick and bony-looking. His eyes were deep-set, and his jaw was huge! He was living under this big tree, and he had the skull of a huge animal stuck on a stick in the ground. I told you what Chief West said about the old man. This has got to be the Neanderthal he was talking about!"

"Okay," she said after a moment. "Let's say I believe you. Where is it that this professor was going with the Neanderthal man?"

"I don't know. But it is possible that if he really had a Neanderthal and was in a wreck, the Neanderthal could make it into the canyon. It opens out onto the coast at the north end of town."

"But where were they going?" repeated Melissa. "What scientific place is around here?"

"What about the Institute of Technology? That's near here. I had a friend whose father worked there. They do a lot of things for the government."

"You're right," she said. A thoughtful look came over her face. "This is wartime. Everything is secret now."

"Maybe," I offered, "the professor was doing some kind of secret experiment with electrical energy. Maybe some kind of death ray or bomb. He said the word *surprise*. Maybe the experiment didn't work the way he thought it would, and it brought a Neanderthal man from the past! It would all fit in, wouldn't it?"

"Yes," agreed Melissa, "and that would mean that nobody knows the caveman's there except you."

"Well," I said, "the chief knows about the caveman."

"No," said Melissa, "he doesn't believe it. And you can't tell him about the Neanderthal because he said that he'd shoot him."

"But if he knew he was really there, he might not."

"Do you want to take the chance and be responsible if something goes wrong?"

Silently, I shook my head.

Melissa continued, "The professor is the only person who can save the Neanderthal from being shot. Leroy, you've always wanted to meet a real, live Neanderthal man. Now's your chance. He's stuck down there until the professor wakes up. He needs a friend!"

"I don't know," I said, feeling a mixture of excitement and fear. "What if the professor had just brought him from the past. What about those broken handcuffs? What if he was wild, and the professor had him drugged or something. He could be dangerous. He was huge. He could rip off my arms and legs like I was a paper doll!"

A gleam came into Melissa's eyes. "Or he could be waiting for a friend. Don't you want to find out?"

"Part of me does, and part of me doesn't," I said unhappily. "I wish there was something else we could do."

"We could put it in the newspapers. Then everybody in town would rush down there, scare the daylights out of him, and he'd be shot for sure!"

"I guess you're right. What's your idea?"

"You had the courage to go down there once."

"What courage? I told you, I had to go down there."

"You could have let them beat you up."

"Right! Sure, Melissa. I just let people beat me up for fun."

"I don't mean exactly that. You could have fought them. I wouldn't go down in that canyon for anything."

"That's different. You're a girl, and your parents are dead, and your grandfather hardly lets you out of his sight anyway."

"All right, Leroy, but I still think you had courage. At least you could hear my idea."

"Okay, I'm listening."

"Food," she said. "There can't be that much to eat down there. Take some food and set it out for him. Hide and watch what happens when he finds it. You could make friends that way."

"I don't know. What if he finds me first?"

There was a soft glow in her eyes. She put her hand on my arm. "You could do it, Leroy."

"Maybe," I said. "I'll think about it. I better get home and clean up before my mother gets there. Promise me you won't say anything to anybody, okay?"

"I'll promise if you'll really think about it. If you could make friends with him, you'd have just what you've dreamed about. After all, how many people get to have their own caveman?"

I couldn't help but grin. "My Neanderthal!"

"Yes, think about it. You might even be famous."

I left her standing by the fence, her eyes still glowing with thoughts of adventure even if she wasn't allowed to participate.

When I got home, I moved quickly. I showered and put my dirty clothes and some others in the washing machine and started it going.

After dinner, I went out to do some weeding on the vegetables in my victory garden. It was a small plot near the backyard water faucet.

When I went back in the house, my mother said, "A few minutes ago, a boy called and asked if you were home. I said that you were working in the garden, but that I could get you. Then he just hung up. Do you have any idea what that's about?"

"Just some joker," I replied. But I thought it was Peanuts or Danny, out to see if I was home.

I didn't say a thing to her about the canyon. I was sure that if I did, she would call up Chief West and that would be it for the Neanderthal.

I went to bed after listening to a Bulldog Drummond mystery on the radio. The window next to my bed was open a few inches and a light breeze blew in. I thought about the caveman and about making friends with him. Wonderful possibilities floated through my mind and with these thoughts I fell asleep.

The Neanderthal and I were walking hand in hand and talking in some unknown language when suddenly a hideous batlike creature came diving at us from out of the sky.

Its mouth opened to expose two rows of deadly, razor-sharp teeth, and from its throat came a piercing wail.

I looked up at the Neanderthal. "What is it?" I asked.

Instead of replying, he faded away and left me sitting upright in my bed.

The wailing continued.

The lighted dial of the clock on my dresser showed that it was 2:25 in the morning.

"Leroy!" came my mother's urgent voice. "It's an air raid. Quick, come into the hallway."

I jumped out of bed and ran through the darkness to her.

"Sit down with me," she said, and we sat together on the floor. She put her arm around me and drew me close to her. "It will be fine," she said. "Don't you worry. It's probably just a false alarm."

"I'm not worried," I said. "I have courage."

"I know you do," she replied. "Maybe I was just reassuring myself."

"You can depend on me," I said, and put my arm around her.

"Good," she said.

The wailing of the sirens continued as we huddled together in the dark, waiting.

And then the guns went off.

THE MYSTERIOUS AIR RAID

"Antiaircraft guns," I said. "There must be unidentified planes up there. Let's go look!"

My mother's arm tightened around me. "No, it's safer to stay here."

"Please, Mom. The ground's not shaking, so no bombs are falling. Let's look out for just a second and see what they're shooting at."

She hesitated.

"They're flying down the coast," I said. "Listen, the guns are following them. Please, Mom, let's look."

"All right," she said.

I slid open the hallway door, and we made our way slowly across the front room to the couch by the window. My mother pulled the cord on the window shade and slowly let it rise.

"Wow!"

The sharp, white light of searchlights cut through the night sky hunting the enemy.

My mother motioned to the left. "Look, that group of lights seems to be focused on something."

The sky around the point where the beams met came alive with the flash of exploding shells.

"Hey," I said pointing to a dark figure on the sidewalk. "It's Doc!" I jumped off the couch, had the front door unlocked, and was outside before she could stop me.

"Hi, Doc!" I called as I ran across the damp lawn in my pajamas and bare feet.

"Leroy, you shouldn't be out here!"

I looked up at the sky. "Did you see them?"

"Well," said Doc, scratching his chin, "I saw something. Whatever they are, they're so high up it's hard to tell."

"You mean they aren't airplanes?"

"At first I thought they were, but then I thought that maybe they were balloons. Just when I was getting a good look at one, shells started exploding all around it and the TNT smoke blotted everything out."

"Maybe whatever it was got blasted out of the sky."

"I don't think so. The searchlights are still coming together in three different places."

For a moment we stood watching the explosions, then suddenly there was a whistling sound. I was just about to say something when Doc grabbed me and shoved me hard toward the lawn.

"Down!" he commanded.

As I toppled forward, I heard something smash into the street.

We both lay on the grass, breathing hard.

The front door opened, and my mother rushed out. "Leroy! Doc! Are you all right?"

Doc got up and reached down for me.

"What happened?" I asked as I got to my feet.

"Shrapnel from a shell, I think," Doc said. "Did I hurt you when I pushed you?"

I moved my arms and legs. "No, I'm fine. How about you?"

"Not so bad for an old man," he replied. "You two go into the house while I find out exactly what that was."

He moved out into the street. From his pocket he withdrew a flashlight with red cellophane over the lens. He knelt down with his back to us. A minute later he was walking back to our door.

"What is it, Doc?"

"It looks like an unexploded shell. I'll have to warn everyone and call the police bomb squad. You stay inside now, Leroy. Promise?"

"Be careful, Doc," said my mother.

"Thank you, Mrs. Penny. I will."

We went back to the window where we could see Doc talking to some of the neighbors across the street.

The firing in our immediate area slowed and stopped, and soon there were just the searchlights crossing, separating, and recrossing.

"The radio!" I said, and jumped off the couch to turn it on. I flipped the switch and the orange dial lit up. Static filled the speaker as I slowly rotated the tuner knob. "Hey, Mom, there's nothing on."

"No," she said. "I remember now that I read that during an air raid, all the stations would go off the air. We'll have to wait for the all clear before we can find out exactly what happened."

I turned the radio off, and we continued to stare out the window.

Within fifteen minutes, a police car arrived and two policemen carefully put up barricades around the shell hole.

A short time later, a small truck with doors in the back and POLICE printed on the sides pulled up by our curb. Two men got out, opened the back of the truck, and removed some equipment, which they took out into the street. The truck completely blocked our view of what was going on.

I yawned and leaned my head against my mother's shoulder.

"I don't imagine we'll see any more," she said. "Do you think you can go back to bed?"

"I guess so."

My bed felt a lot better than I thought it would. "I suppose we'll find out what's going on in the morning."

"Yes," she said. "Whatever the guns were shooting at is not around here anymore." She leaned over and kissed me on the forehead. "See if you can get some sleep now."

"Okay." I rolled over and listened to the sounds coming in the open window by my bed. I heard what I thought was the deep thundering of guns far to the south.

The voices of the policemen on the street drifted back to me, but they were mixed and blurred. I moved to the edge of my bed closest to the window and concentrated with all my might. Instead of unscrambling their voices, I fell asleep.

The all-clear sirens woke me at seven in the morning.

The first thing I did was to look out the window by my bed. I had a good view of the vacant lot next door. It was empty and weedy. Nothing had changed. I wanted to see the shattered wing of a Japanese bomber, or a torn tail section, or—something! But everything was just the same.

Then I remembered the shell in the street. Quickly, I grabbed a pair of pants, pulled them on over my pajamas, and made a dash for the front door.

"Leroy?" came my mother's sleepy voice from her bedroom.

She was too late. I was out the door and into the street. But again, I felt nothing but dismay. The shell was gone! The hole was filled up and waiting for a new coat of asphalt to make what happened there all but invisible.

From my position in the middle of the street, I looked about the block and found nothing changed anywhere. Not one sign of the night's excitement. Air raids were, I was sure, supposed to provide some sort of visible change to the landscape, to the people.

I walked back to my house and went inside.

"Leroy?"

"Yes, Mom?"

The bathroom door opened, and she came out wearing her pink bathrobe. Her long black hair was pulled back and held with a clip.

"What did you see?"

"Nothing! The shell's gone, and there's nothing different anywhere."

"Why don't you turn on the radio. Maybe we can get some news."

I turned on the radio, but the stations were still off the air.

"We'll have breakfast and get some chores done," she said, "and we'll try again at eight o'clock."

At eight our luck changed.

"This is Bill Wallington with the morning news. Antiaircraft guns thundered over the Los Angeles area today for the first time in the war, but hours later what they were shooting at remains a military secret.

"An unidentified object moving slowly down the coast from Santa Monica was reported by some as a balloon and by others as an airplane. Some observers claimed to have seen two planes over Long Beach.

"Army intelligence scoffed at reports by civilian observers that as many as two hundred planes were over the area.

"In San Francisco, the Western Defense Command announced that no bombs were dropped and no planes were shot down during the antiaircraft firing in the Los Angeles area.

"The Defense Command stated that although our planes are, at this moment, still surveying the area, it appears that last night's supposed air threat was just a false alarm.

"And now in other news—"

I turned off the radio and looked at my mother. "Does that mean that all those guns were shooting at nothing?"

"No," she said. "It means that whatever was up there dropped no bombs and did no damage. But the army and navy may know more than they are willing to tell us."

"Doc told me he saw something in the searchlights. I believe him."

"He's usually very reliable. I'm sure he saw something. The question is what? Maybe we'll find out in the next few days."

"I'd like to go up and talk to him."

My mother started filling up the sink with water.

"That's fine for later. It's too early for you to be up there now. You stick around this morning and help me clean up the house and the yard. I have classes at the studio this afternoon. You can visit Doc then."

"Okay," I said. "I'll start by taking out the trash."

At 1:15, I rang Doc's doorbell.

The curtain at the front window was pulled back a bit and Melissa peeked out. Then the front door was unlocked and opened.

"Where's Doc?" I asked.

"He had to go to a meeting of Air Raid Wardens. He'll be back in an hour."

"Did he say anything about last night?"

"He told me about you and the shell. I'll bet that was scary."

"Not really. I didn't know what was going on until it was over. The news on the radio said the whole thing was a false alarm."

She nodded. "Doc says that maybe it was and maybe it wasn't. He has two ideas. One is that maybe an army weather balloon got away and drifted down the coast. He said that after the big air raid it caused, the army might be embarrassed to say anything public about it."

"What's the other?"

"The other is that maybe a Japanese submarine lying off the coast released those balloons. While the city was involved in an air raid, they could sneak those three German saboteurs onto shore."

"Which idea does he believe the most?" I asked.

"He didn't say. But he is sure that before the shell smoke clouded the sky, he saw a balloon. He doesn't think there were any airplanes at all."

"So the Germans could be in town right now!"

"Or it could have been an army balloon. Don't forget that, Leroy."

"I know, but still . . . I'd like to have seen a Japanese bomber get shot down."

Melissa frowned. "But that would mean that we had really been attacked. You wouldn't want that, would you?"

"I guess not."

"Anyway, if we had been attacked, you wouldn't be able to see the Neanderthal man today."

During the air raid, I had been more excited than scared. And I had forgotten all about my caveman. Now I thought of him again, and I was more scared than excited.

"Look, Melissa. At first Doc thought he saw planes. Now he thinks they were balloons. Maybe all I saw was a bum."

"That's not true, Leroy. You couldn't have convinced me if it wasn't true. You crossed your heart!"

"Melissa . . ."

"Come into the kitchen," she said sternly. "I've made up a food pack for you to take to the Neanderthal." She turned her back and walked briskly into the kitchen, confident that I would follow her.

I did.

7

THE MEETING

"You there, where are you going?"

I stopped and turned.

The man had just backed his car out of his garage. He was leaning out the window and staring at me.

"I was going to look at the canyon."

He shook his head. "The canyon is a dangerous place. You stay away from there."

"But I was just going to see what it looked like."

"You must be new in town. See that sign over there? It says, No Trespassing. You go over and read that sign, and stay away from the canyon. Find your fun someplace else. All right?"

"Yes, sir."

He watched as I walked toward the sign.

Most grown-ups let you alone if you went over and looked at the canyon. A few acted like they were your parents.

I stopped in front of the sign and pretended to read. That must have satisfied him. I heard his car start up, and when I turned around he was gone.

Quickly, I doubled back, trotted across the field, and stepped over the rim at the exact spot where I had entered the canyon the day before.

I descended about ten feet, grabbed the twisted branch of a tree to stop myself, and sat down.

I looked at the brown paper bag in my hand. Melissa's offering to the caveman consisted of two apples, a banana, and two cold hot dogs.

"I don't know," I'd said to Melissa. "This whole thing might not be such a good idea. What if he's mean?"

"We've already gone over this. If he was mean he would have come after you. You said so yourself. You can make friends with him, Leroy. I know you can!"

"I wish I was as sure as you are."

"Oh, Leroy! If Doc wasn't going to be back here soon, I'd leave you here and go myself."

"There's no chance of that, and you know it!"

She gave me the coldest stare I had ever seen. "If you really think that, then you can go out of the front door and don't ever come back here again!"

"Oh, come on, Melissa!"

"Oh, come on, yourself, Leroy. Tell me that you really and truly don't have any desire to meet an actual Neanderthal man."

"You know I do, but . . ."

"But nothing!"

Besides taking the food, Melissa had come up with another idea.

"You'll make a drawing," she said. "It will be like a cartoon in the papers. The first picture will have a boy handing a caveman an apple. The second picture will have the caveman eating the apple, and the third picture will show the caveman and the boy shaking hands."

"That's stupid!" I said.

"Then you think of a better way to tell him you want to be friends."

I tried, but I couldn't. When the drawing was done, I had folded it and put it inside the bag.

"I wish I could go with you," Melissa said as I left.

"I do too," I replied.

I sighed and looked down the canyon wall. No one was throwing dirt clods at me now. I could take my time and pick an easier route. I took the paper bag, pulled the top of it under my belt, and tightened the belt one notch. The bag hung securely, and both my hands were free.

Slowly and carefully, with one eye always on the canyon below me, I climbed down to the bottom.

My shoes filled up with dirt, just like the day before, so I sat down and emptied them out.

From now on, I had to move like an Indian—no stepping on twigs that would snap and no panicking at dead birds or lizards.

I found the first tree I had been under and ducked under its branches. I moved quietly, following my earlier path. I saw no one. I closed my eyes and listened for human sounds. I heard nothing.

Moving from bush to bush, tree to tree, my heart thudding in my chest, I made my way carefully toward the Neanderthal's tree.

Once, I cracked a twig that was hidden under some leaves. I froze and didn't move again for a full minute. Every step I took was carefully planned, and every bush and tree carefully examined.

I was fearful that at any moment the Neanderthal would pounce on me and tear me limb from limb.

About thirty feet from the willow was a small pine tree with branches that came out of it like wagon spokes. On the side of the pine closest to the willow was a large, green bush. It was made up of soft stalks with long, pointed leaves.

I moved carefully up to the pine tree, stepped over and ducked under its branches, and crouched behind the bush.

For the next five minutes, I sat in a cramped position looking through a small opening in the bush. No sounds came from the tree. I was convinced the Neanderthal was not there.

Loosening my belt, I removed the bag and held it in my right hand. Then, moving as quietly as I could, I approached the tree.

With shaking hands, I opened the bag and spilled out its contents. I opened the drawing, set the food out as planned, and then backed slowly away from the willow. All the time I was moving backward, I never took my eyes from the food and the willow.

When I reached the bush, I felt my way around it with my left hand. I backed right over to the spot where I could see through to the tree. My view was perfect. I could see the food lying on the ground as well as the area to the right and left of it.

I stared so hard at the Neanderthal's tree that my vision began to blur. Closing my eyes, I put my hands behind me and leaned back.

Instead of a pine branch, I felt something firm and warm.

A chill went through me and my legs began to shake. My imagination told me that the Neanderthal man had been watching me all along. When I had gone to put out the food, he had taken my place behind the bush. And he was behind me right now.

I leaned forward and prayed rapidly. "Please, God, this is Leroy in the canyon. I know it's wartime and lots of people are praying to you, but please, I'm in terrible trouble, and I need your help. Please, God, if you could just let it be my imagination this one time, I promise I won't bother you again for the entire war. Thank you, God. A-men!"

I turned slowly around, opened my eyes, and found myself looking at—a pine tree! I breathed the greatest sigh of relief the world has ever known. It was my imagination after all.

Reaching out with both hands, I grabbed a nearby limb and squeezed it. It was wonderfully real!

"Thank you, God," I said out loud. "Thank you! Thank You!"

A very deep voice came from behind me. *"Th-ank . . . you!"*

I whirled around and found myself looking up into a black beard, large nostrils, and piercing eyes.

"AHHHH—!"

A giant hand clapped over my face and cut off my cry and my air.

The Neanderthal stepped out from behind the bush and held me up as if I was nothing more than a piece of straw.

I was eyeball-to-eyeball with him. It was just what I had always wanted. And now I was done for!

I thought of my mother, I thought of Doc, and I thought of Melissa who had been so sure of herself.

Then everything started to spin, and I fainted.

The next thing I knew, I was lying on my back on the hard ground. I blinked twice, opened my eyes wide, and found myself looking up into clear, blue sky.

Something cold and damp was on my forehead. I reached my hand up and pulled off a couple of large, wet leaves. I sat up and found that I was next to a small stream. The water was cool and clear, and when I drank some it revived me.

But where was the Neanderthal? I looked around but could not see him. Maybe he had just gone to his tree to get something, and he was on his way back.

That thought scared me. I didn't want to see him again, at least not right that minute. I wanted time to think this whole thing over and talk to Melissa again.

Quickly and quietly, I headed across the canyon toward the spot where I had come down.

Willie Owens stared at me through eyes magnified by his glasses. "It's fantastic! It's terrific! Of course you've got to go again. There's no doubt about it, Leroy. And you've got to go tomorrow."

"I was thinking more like next weekend."

"Absolutely not! It's out of the question. The Neanderthal expects to see you again tomorrow. I'm sure of it. You've got to take more food and go back down tomorrow!"

"I don't know," I said. "Tomorrow is Sunday. I won't be able to sneak any food out from under my mother, and I know that Melissa will have trouble with Doc being there all day."

"No problem," Willie said. "My parents are going to the movies tomorrow afternoon. Doc already told them that he'd look in on me, so I know he'd let Melissa come over. We can use my place as a base. I can even supply the food. This is going to be neat!"

"Yeah, but I'm still the one who has to go down there."

"No, Leroy, you're the lucky one. You *get* to go down there. I mean, he didn't hurt you, and he even spoke!"

"But that could have just been imitation, like a parrot."

"It could be, but I'm betting it's not. Anyway, we'll find out tomorrow!"

Willie's enthusiasm swept away a lot of my doubts and fears.

"I'm glad I came over today," I said. "When Melissa wasn't at home, I didn't know what to do. I wanted to talk to you, only I wasn't sure whether you'd believe me."

"Heck yes. It's absolutely, scientifically possible for something like this to happen." He leaned forward. "Look, Leroy, comic-book cavemen are all right, but they're made up. I read something else. Let me show you."

He propelled himself across the room to some bookshelves and began flipping through a stack of comics.

"Here it is!" he announced as he yanked one from the middle of the stack. He pushed himself back and held up the book.

On the cover was a death ray shooting at a rocket ship.

"Willie, that's just another comic book."

"No it's not. Look at the title, 'Future Science Fantasies.' It's the word *science* that counts. The people who write this can predict future inventions and everything. They have one-page articles by real scientists inside."

He flipped some pages and stopped. "Here's the one I was looking for. It's called 'Space Travel—Time Travel.' It says that first men will use rocket ships to travel in space. Later on, they'll use a machine that will break down their bodies into atoms and shoot them through space to wherever they want to be."

"No kidding?"

He held up the article for me to inspect.

"That's why I believe you, Leroy. I think the professor's invention must have reached into the past, broken down this Neanderthal's body into atoms and transported them here." He closed the magazine. "You can count on me. I'll help you, and I won't tell a soul."

"Thanks, Willie. I better get home now. I'll talk to Melissa later and let you know if it's all right for tomorrow."

"Before you leave," he said reaching into his pocket, "take this." He held out his hand containing the Indian head penny.

"That's your lucky penny. I can't take that, Willie. It's going to help you walk again."

"Leroy, if this penny is going to bring anybody luck, it's going to be you. Before you go to sleep tonight, hold the coin between both hands, and close your eyes. Rub your hands back and forth to heat up the coin, and make a wish. Sleep with it under your pillow, and keep it with you all day tomorrow."

I took the penny and held it tightly in my fist. "Thanks, Willie, I'll do it."

We opened his bedroom door and he wheeled himself into the front room. I said good-bye to him and walked down his front steps and over to the curb.

"See you tomorrow, Leroy!" he called.

I turned to wave and saw him sitting behind the screen door. He raised his right hand, and with his first two fingers made the sign V for victory.

That night, when I was in bed, I took the Indian head from under my pillow. I held it between both palms and rubbed hard.

I had already prayed that day. While my prayer hadn't exactly been answered the way I meant, I was still alive. Maybe my wish stood a chance. If it did, I would make it a good one. Melissa and Willie would be included.

Closing my eyes tightly, I said, "Whoever is out there listening to wishes, this is Leroy on Twenty-second Street, and this is my wish . . ."

THE LAND OF THE DEAD

"Hello?"

"Is that you, Bullslinger?"

The phone had rung as I was getting ready to leave for Willie's.

I sighed, "What do you want, Peanuts?"

"Just this, Bullslinger. For my money, going down in the canyon doesn't mean hiding under the first tree you come to and then sneaking out as fast as you can."

"That's not what happened."

"Don't gimme that! You streaked out of there as soon as we left."

"How do you know what I did if you were gone?"

" 'Cause of the way you ran after school. I think

Danny's right. I think you're a creepy little coward. You got lucky, you know that? If it wasn't for some old coot who thought he owned the place we'd have stayed around a lot longer."

"So, that's not my fault. I came back looking for you later. I could have used your help."

"What's this, Bullslinger, another story?"

"Never mind."

"Don't 'never mind' me, Bullslinger. I'll see you at school tomorrow. I want to hear this one, and it better be good. If it's not, we'll get you after school and pants you right in front of everyone on the playground."

He hung up and left me looking into the mouthpiece of the phone.

I was angry, but there wasn't much I could do about it then. Peanuts would have to wait until Monday.

Willie's parents had invited my mother to go to the movies with them, and they had left fifteen minutes ago.

I locked the front door and headed across the street.

"Okay," Willie said checking the contents of the bag. "An apple, a peeled orange, two pieces of fried chicken, and some buttered bread. That's a healthy meal."

"You're all ready to go," said Melissa.

Willie handed me the bag. "Got the Indian head?"

I reached into my pocket and held it up. "For good luck!"

There was an awkward period of silence where we just stared at each other.

"I wish you could both come with me."

Willie put his right hand down on his leg and rubbed it. "I wish we could come too."

Melissa's eyes flashed. "I want to go! I'm getting tired of Doc always keeping me around home. I can never do anything."

"He doesn't mean anything bad," I said. "My mom says he's overprotective right now, but he'll change."

"I may run away some day."

"You don't mean that."

"Yes, I do. He wouldn't let me go to Susan Butterfield's birthday party. It was down at the amusement pier. He said some of the rides were dangerous. Everybody who went had a good time, and nobody got hurt." She stood up. "I'll go with you today!"

"Please, Melissa, you promised you'd help out here. Doc is coming over to check. If he finds you're gone, Willie will have to tell him what's going on, and that will ruin everything."

"Oh . . . all right," she said, "but I want to see the Neanderthal for myself. Promise me, Leroy, that before anything happens to him, you'll take me to see him myself."

"I promise."

"Cross your heart and hope to die!"

"I promised. What do you want?"

"You didn't sound like you meant it. Cross your heart and hope to die, or I'm going with you today!"

Willie laughed. "Go on, Leroy."

I ran my finger over my chest in an exaggerated motion.

"Cross my heart and hope to die if I don't take Melissa to see the Neanderthal before Chief West or anybody else takes him away. There, are you satisfied?"

"Satisfied," she said.

"Remember, you can't stay too long," said Willie. "You need to be back by four o'clock."

"Here goes then," I said and started toward the door.

"Wait!" cried Melissa.

"What's wrong?"

"You can't go out the front door, Doc could see you. Go out the back and down the alley. When Doc comes over to check on us, I'll meet him at the front porch and tell him everything is all right."

"See," I said, "that's why we need you here today."

She made a face at me.

I left Willie at the back door and Melissa at the back gate.

A half an hour later, I was there. I didn't see any grown-ups around, so I went straight across the field and down into the canyon.

This time, I wouldn't try to hide. I would make

my way as easily as I could to the Neanderthal's tree, take out some food so he could see it, and tell him I was there.

That was the plan. I was scared, but two things kept me going. First, I really wanted to talk to the Neanderthal. Second, I had to prove to myself that I wasn't a coward. If I could do that, I could face Peanuts at school.

Carefully, I made my way back to his tree. Every so often, I'd stop and listen, but other than the chirp of a bird or the buzz of a fly, I heard nothing.

Finally, the tree was in front of me. I took a deep breath and walked up to it.

It was like being at home plate with the bases loaded. If I had been playing baseball at school, I would have struck out and Danny Davis would be after me. But I was not at school, and I was determined not to strike out this time.

Food in hand, I stood facing the Neanderthal's tree.

"Hello?" My voice came out high and squeaky. I cleared my throat and tried again. "Hello?" This time it sounded more like me.

Nothing happened. Was he there? I looked hard at the tree wishing I had Superman's X-ray vision.

Then the deep voice came from inside the tree. "Thank you! Thank you!"

The branches parted, and he stepped out. In his right hand was the club with the stone in it. He walked toward me until he was no more than three feet away.

My legs shook like Jell-O, but I kept them together and stood my ground.

"Food?" I asked and held out the apple.

He looked me up and down several times before he focused on the apple. "Food," he repeated and took the apple from my hand.

He gave it a squeeze, sniffed it, and with his massive jaws crunched the apple to bits, core and all.

Before he was finished, I had the chicken out. He devoured that and everything else. Melissa had been so right about the food.

I reached in my back pocket and pulled out another drawing of the Neanderthal and the boy shaking hands. I held it up to him.

"Friends?" I said.

He took the drawing from me and wrinkled his forehead as he studied it. After a moment, he turned and walked toward his tree. When he got there, he pushed the branches back and motioned for me to enter.

As I walked past him he said, "Boy and Ooma friends."

I jumped a foot!

"Ooma frighten boy?"

"No," I said, but I took two steps away from him. "You . . . you can talk!"

"Yes. Professor Ludlow teach Ooma talk." He

looked around. "Where Professor Ludlow now?" He shook his head. "Professor and Ooma together. Then Ooma wake up here. Professor no come. Boy come instead." He pressed his fingertips against his forehead as though it would help him remember something. "Professor make new science machine bring Ooma from long ago. Professor say many people want hear Ooma's story."

"Could you tell your story to me?"

Ooma considered this for a moment, nodded, and sat down on the ground. I sat opposite him.

"Professor Ludlow say machine bring Ooma from fifty thousand years ago."

"Then you are a Neanderthal!" I said in awe.

He nodded. "Professor say Ooma Neanderthal man. Live fifty thousand years ago."

"Did the professor say where?"

"Professor call place Europe. Between England and France. Land then. Water now. If machine not bring, Ooma be in Land of Dead."

"You mean that you were about to be killed?"

"Ooma fight cave bear."

I sat forward. "Did the bear attack you?"

He nodded. "Make smoke in cave where bear sleep. Bear come out angry. Hunters fight with spears and stones."

"How did he get you?"

"Friend slip on rock. Ooma reach down, pull him back. Bear turn on Ooma and hit with paw. Knock

Ooma down. Ooma see teeth of bear. Feel breath of bear on face. Then feel ground open up and world become black. Ooma think he fall into Land of Dead!"

"But you didn't die. The time machine got you!"

He shook his head, pulled his thick eyebrows together, and spoke slowly. "When Ooma stop falling, he in Professor Ludlow's laboratory . . . in 1942!"

AN UNEXPECTED TURN OF EVENTS

"What happened when you got there?" I asked.

"Not remember well." He pointed to the tree. "Since Ooma wake up here, have pain come in head." He stopped and looked at me. "Why professor leave Ooma alone?"

My mind raced. Should I tell him about the accident or not? If I did, he might want to see the professor. That would mean leaving the canyon. I'd never be able to control what happened then.

"I don't know why he left you," I said. "He must have had some reason. Maybe he had to go back to the laboratory for something. Do you remember anything about where the laboratory was?"

He closed his eyes tightly and gave his head a

shake. "At night have dream of travel with professor. Only remember dream."

"Well . . . I understand how you must feel. I got chased down here by some guys who don't like me. I sure felt alone then."

Ooma looked at me for a moment, then he said, "Why run? Think Ooma hurt boy?"

"Me? Did I think you'd hurt me?" I repeated, stalling my answer. "I didn't know who you were. I didn't know how you'd act."

He didn't reply right away, but the expression on his face was not one of anger. I relaxed and waited for him to speak.

"One winter, when Ooma boy, father sent to Land of Dead. Snow come down mountain and bury father and other hunters. Soon, mother sick. She go to Land of Dead to join father."

"I'm sorry," I said.

He raised his hand. "Other hunters, other mothers take care of Ooma. People long ago not hurt each other."

"But what if someone hit you first?"

"Hit back hard!"

"I understand," I said. "It's pretty much the same now."

"Why boys chase you?"

"Because of a game we play. I'm not very good at it. I do things wrong, and we lose. I bet you were pretty good at your games, though."

"Ooma play hunting games with other boys. Not throw spear good when small. Only later, when big. Then Ooma throw spear good."

"Did you ever have any enemies, boys who didn't like you? Did you get into fights?"

He smiled at me, and his large teeth seemed to gleam. "Many fights! Sometime Ooma win. Many times when small, Ooma lose."

"Maybe I'll get better when I get older," I said. "It wouldn't be so bad if I knew I would. One thing for sure, I'd like to end up as big as you."

"Ooma big, but that not help now."

"No," I said, "I guess it doesn't, does it? Could you tell me what life was like when you were small?"

He smiled, squinted his eyes, and looked down at his fingers. He began to move them one at a time, and then he stopped.

He looked up at me and said, "Professor teach Ooma count, but not remember all numbers. Boy help Ooma remember." He began holding up the fingers on his hand.

I counted. "Five, ten, fifteen, twenty, twenty-five."

"Twenty-five!" his voice boomed out. Twenty-five in tribe. Live together in cave in winter. Very cold time. Professor Ludlow call Age of Ice. Tribe cover front of cave. Make fire inside. Sometime hungry."

"What about summer?" I asked.

"Summer good time. Tribe leave cave. Follow animals. Many deer." He waved his arms about. "Very big animal like cattle. Also woolly rhino."

"You ate a woolly rhino?"

His mouth drew back and his teeth gleamed. "Eat heart of rhino. Give Ooma courage!" He tapped his head. "Eat brain of rhino. Help Ooma know rhino. Make easy to hunt!"

My stomach felt funny at the thought of that. "Did you eat anything else?"

"Eat heart and brain of cave bear. Eat heart and brain of woolly mammoth!"

"Did you eat the heart and brain of everything?"

"Not frog! Ooma not like frog. Boy like frog?"

My insides gave a little jump, and I looked around. Was he going to feed me a frog in return for what I'd given him? I didn't want to be rude, but I definitely didn't want to eat a frog.

"Not talk," said Ooma. "Not like frog?"

I hesitated. "Actually . . . no."

He looked about. "That good. No frog here."

What a relief! I smiled. "Could you tell me more about your life?"

For the next hour, he continued to tell me about the tribal life of the Neanderthals. He told me of the way they painted themselves before a hunt and showed me a dance they did when they were successful. He told of hunts where they drove large animals over the edge of cliffs in order to kill them. I envied their bravery in facing danger with just spears, clubs, and rocks.

Finally, I knew I had to get back. "I want to go and talk to my friends about you," I said. "Maybe they can help. You stay here. You'll be safe, and the professor might come. I'll be back tomorrow, and I'll bring more food."

He nodded. "Ooma wait for boy."

I pointed to my chest. "Leroy."

"Leeee-roy," he repeated slowly. "Le-roy friend."

I said good-bye to him and headed toward the canyon wall.

"We've got to find out how Professor Ludlow is doing," declared Willie. "But we sure can't talk to the chief. What can we do?"

We both looked at Melissa. "Well," she said, "there are only two hospitals in town. Let's call them."

"Can we do that?" I said, amazed at so simple a solution.

"We can try," she answered.

"Who will talk?" I asked.

"I can make my voice low if I speak softly," said Willie.

We went over to the phone, and Willie held it so we could hear.

"Good afternoon, Saint John's Hospital."

"Good afternoon," said Willie. "I wanted to find out if Professor Ludlow is a patient there."

"Just one moment, and I'll connect you to the Patient Desk."

We heard ringing. Then, "Patient Desk."

Willie repeated his question.

"No, I'm sorry. We have no Ludlow listed here."

"Thank you," said Willie. He hung up, then lifted the phone and dialed again.

A crisp voice answered on the second ring. "Santa Monica Hospital."

Again we were connected to the Patient Desk, and after a moment's hesitation the woman said, "Yes, he is a patient here."

We stared at each other. Willie, totally unsure of what to do next, looked at Melissa for help.

"Ask if you can talk to him," she whispered.

"Can I talk to the professor, please?" Willie said.

"I'm sorry," said the woman. "He has been in a coma since his automobile accident. We've been trying to locate his family. Are you a family member?"

"No," said Willie, and added, "thank you," and hung up.

"Well, that answers our question," said Melissa.

"What do we do now?" I asked.

At that moment, a car pulled into the driveway.

"Our parents are back," I said.

"Look," said Willie, "let's keep him hidden, keep feeding him, and hope the professor gets better in the next couple of days."

"If he doesn't get better fast, I think we should try to explain things to Chief West," I said. "I wouldn't want Ooma to wander up here on his own. He'd really get hurt then."

"What's Chief West going to do?" asked Willie. "Professor Ludlow is the key to everything. Without him to explain things, the chief might shoot the Neanderthal, or put him in jail, or in the zoo! He'll die there. The Neanderthal's at home where he is, Leroy. Wait a couple of days."

"Okay" I said. "We'll wait until Tuesday. If he's not better then, I'm for telling the chief."

"The lucky penny has worked so far," said Willie. "Give it a chance, Leroy."

I had forgotten all about the penny. I reached into my pocket and felt for it. It was still there. "A couple of days," I repeated.

The car's doors slammed. We heard my mother and Willie's parents walking up the front steps.

"Hi, kids!" called Willie's dad.

"Hi!" we replied.

"Well," said Willie's mom, "were you three bored to death this afternoon?"

"Not hardly!" exclaimed Willie. Then, catching our looks he added, "There were some good shows on the radio!"

The next morning I awoke and thought about Peanuts. Besides playing sick and staying home, how could I avoid him?

I pulled open a drawer and took out my marble bag. I hadn't played marbles in a week. The marble area was under some trees on the lower part of the playground. It was a place to hide without hiding.

Charlie, the German Ace, had looked hopeful but soon settled for the marble game.

It was a good idea, and it saved me during recess. But when I left the room at lunch, they were all waiting for me at the classroom door.

"Win any marbles, Bullslinger?" asked Peanuts.

"We saw you coming from there," added Nick.

Peanuts folded his arms across his chest and snapped, "You better have a good story or you know what's gonna happen!"

Nick leaned forward and whispered, "You're gonna get pantsed in front of the girls!"

"I've got a story," I replied.

"We're going to the cafeteria," said Peanuts. "We'll meet you at the handball courts in twenty minutes. Don't try to hide either!"

Twenty minutes later, I stood backed into a corner of one of the courts.

"Let's hear it, Bullslinger!" said Peanuts coldly.

"All right," I replied. "What I'm going to tell you is true. It's what really happened to me after you left me in the canyon. Whether you believe it or not is your business, but I'm saying it's true."

"You're stalling," sneered Danny. "You don't have anything to say."

I fixed him with as serious a look as I could. "There's a Neanderthal man living down in the canyon. I've seen him, and I've talked to him."

"Now that," declared Peanuts, "is *real* bull! Go

on, Bullslinger. You may get yourself out of this yet."

I told them everything that happened. I left out nothing. I did it because I figured that they'd never believe me. And they didn't. At least, not at first.

"Pretty good!" said Peanuts when I'd finished. "I got to admit, you're the best bullslinger in this whole school. What do you say, Marty?"

"It was a good story," he said flatly.

Danny Davis looked sullenly at the ground. "What a bunch of garbage!"

Peanuts gave me a scowl. "We ain't forgetting how you tried to run the other day. From now on, when we want a story, you deliver. Don't forget! You're off the hook now, so scram!"

"Wait!" cried Nick. "I want my story tomorrow, and it better be a good one."

"Sure, Nick," I replied, and walked away.

There were ten minutes left of lunch, so I went down to the marble area and watched the end of a game that I wished I'd been in.

By the end of the school day, I'd managed to put Peanuts out of my mind and was again making plans to take food to the Neanderthal.

The final bell rang, I got my books together, and made my way out of the room.

"Bullslinger!"

Peanuts, Danny, Nick, and Marty stood smiling at me.

"I just told you a story at lunch," I said. "I don't have to tell Nick's until tomorrow."

"We don't want a story," replied Peanuts. "We want you to take us down in the canyon to meet the Neanderthal."

"But that was just a story," I said.

"You swore to us it was true!" said Danny.

"Yeah," added Nick, "so we want to meet this guy. If we don't, if you lied to us, then we're gonna pants you in the canyon and let you walk home that way!"

"But the canyon is a dangerous place," I protested. "Nobody goes into the canyon. That old man will chase us away."

"He can't chase us away if he's not there," replied Peanuts.

"If he is," said Nick, "we'll go down someplace else."

"Right," agreed Danny. "And we know the canyon used to be dangerous, but if it's still dangerous then how come a little goon like you can go in and not get hurt? If you can do it, so can we!"

I turned to Marty, but he looked away.

"Come on," said Peanuts grabbing my arm. "Let's get moving. Can't keep that caveman waiting!"

10

PANTSED

As we walked along, I reached deep into my pants pocket for the Indian head penny. Rubbing it between my thumb and forefinger, I made a wish.

"Please," I thought, "let the old man be there and chase us away!"

Peanuts seemed excited and kept up a constant stream of chatter.

"What are you gonna do when you meet the caveman?" he asked Nick.

"I'm gonna ask him if he had to go to school. If he didn't, I'm gonna ask him to adopt me."

"What about you, Danny, what are you gonna ask the caveman?"

Danny gave me a cold smile. "I'm gonna find out

if he can play baseball with his club. If he can, I'm gonna let him have batting practice on Bullslinger's head!"

When we arrived at the field, the streets were deserted. The old man was nowhere to be seen. The Indian head penny had let me down.

I felt panicky. What if I'd picked the wrong penny off my dresser in the morning?

I dug my hand into my pocket, fumbled with the coin, and pulled it out. There was the profile of the Indian chief.

"Get movin', Bullslinger!" ordered Peanuts.

I glanced again at the coin. Maybe it only worked if you rubbed it between your palms. I put my palms together.

"What are you playing with that penny for?" growled Peanuts. "Give it here!"

"It's nothing," I said and quickly stuffed it in my pocket.

He made a fist. "Gimme!"

I took it out and handed it to him. He examined it carefully.

"This is nothing but an old Indian head cent. I'd rather have a Lincoln any day." He flipped it back to me. "Get going," he ordered.

I dropped the coin into my pocket and headed toward the canyon rim. As I walked, I rubbed my hand over the outside of my pocket and felt the penny. Maybe just having it on me would help a little.

"Now let's see your caveman," said Peanuts as he started down the canyon side.

"He better be real," warned Nick, "or you're gonna get it good!"

"Remember," said Peanuts. "We have to be fair to Bullslinger, here. He gets his chance before we pants him."

As soon as we reached the bottom, Danny looked around and said, "It was just a story. Going through all these trees and bushes is a waste of time. Let's pants him right now and get out of here."

Nick grabbed me around the waist and hoisted me up. "Come on, Danny, here he is. Strip 'em off."

"Let me go!" I cried.

Peanuts glowered at them. "What's the matter with you two? You're not scared of this place, are you?"

"Heck no!" blustered Danny.

" 'Course not," mumbled Nick and let me go.

"Which way?" asked Peanuts.

"Follow me," I said and began moving, but not in the direction of the Neanderthal's tree.

I led them back and forth across the canyon while I tried to figure out what I could do. I did not want to share the Neanderthal with them.

"Ouch!" hollered Peanuts as the spikes on a thorny vine scratched his arm. "If we don't get to that tree quick, I'm gonna let Nick have you now!"

I definitely did not want to get pantsed. I led them to the tree.

"That's it," I said. "You better let me go first." I started forward.

"Don't let him!" hissed Danny.

Peanuts grabbed my arm and yanked me back. "We stay together, Bullslinger!"

The four of us walked to the edge of the large bush.

"Ooma," I said loudly, "Leroy here with friends."

Nothing happened.

"Hey, caveman," hollered Peanuts. "You better come out or we're gonna pants your friend Bullslinger. You hear that?"

"Ah," said Danny disgustedly, "we all knew it was a lie."

"It isn't a lie," I said. "Come into the tree with me, and I'll show you."

Danny turned to Peanuts. "I don't trust him. It's some kind of a trick."

"What trick?" replied Peanuts. "We got him four to one down here. What can he do?"

Danny looked around. "I don't know, but I don't like this too much. He's been down here before, and we haven't."

Peanuts sneered. "You *are* scared to be down here, aren't you, Danny? Bullslinger's got more guts than you have!"

"I'm not saying I'm afraid," Danny protested. "I'm just saying that I don't trust him."

"Then you grab one of his arms, and I'll grab the other. That way we got control of him."

"That's good enough for me," replied Danny and gripped me tightly.

"Look at that!" exclaimed Nick as we stepped inside the tree.

Peanuts let go of my arm and walked over to examine the skull. "Not bad!" he said. "I got to hand it to you, Bullslinger. You set this up pretty good."

"What do you mean 'set it up'?"

"I mean that you not only thought up the story, you found this old dog's skull and stuck it down here to make the whole thing look real."

"What!" I cried. "Are you serious? You're telling me that *I* did this?"

Peanuts laughed. "You're a good actor too. Sure, we believed you came down here. But we never believed there was any Neanderthal man down here. What do you take us for, a bunch of birdbrains?"

"Now, Peanuts?" blurted out Nick.

"Sure," replied Peanuts. "Let's pants him now!"

"Look!" I yelled. "There's the Neanderthal!"

"Huh?" said Danny and looked where I'd pointed.

I whirled around, broke free of his grasp, and ran out of the tree.

Peanuts's voice exploded behind me. "After him! Don't let him get away!"

"Around that bush!" hollered Nick. "He ran around that bush!"

"You go that way, I'll go the other!" directed Danny.

I burst out of the bush and headed into some trees.

"There he goes!" yelled Peanuts. "Follow me."

I heard the crunch of his footsteps behind me.

"Peanuts, over here!" cried Danny.

"Coming!" yelled Peanuts.

"I see him," panted Nick. "I'll get him!"

To my right was a thicket of underbrush and small bushes. I plunged into it and began pushing my way through thin twisted branches.

"This way!" yelled Nick.

"There!" cried Peanuts. "He's in there."

I lifted my leg, twisted over some branches, and felt a sharp pain in my leg. A broken branch had cut through my pants leg and was holding me fast.

Marty's calm voice came from behind me. "We got him. He's caught in there."

He was right.

Peanuts and Danny held me fast.

"Thought you'd get away, huh, Bullslinger?" said Peanuts. "Well you never stood a chance!"

"Right," panted Nick. "We had you all the time."

"Let's take more than his pants," said Danny. "Let's leave him in his birthday suit!"

That was too much for me. I screamed as loud as I could. *"Ooma, help! Ooma, Leroy need help!"*

Peanuts laughed. "Give it up, Bullslinger. It's all over but the pantsing."

"Ooma! Help! Ooma!"

Peanuts looked at Nick. "Lift him up, Nick."

"I been waiting for this," said Nick moving behind me and wrapping his arms around my chest.

"Ooma! Leroy need help!"

Peanuts grabbed at my waist and started undoing my pants.

"Get his shoes off," said Danny.

"Got 'em," said Marty.

I felt my pants coming down. "Stop it!"

Danny laughed. "Tough luck, Bullslinger."

Suddenly a deep voice bellowed, *"Ooma help friend Leroy!"*

"Huh?" said Danny.

"What's that?" asked a startled Peanuts.

Ooma charged around a tree with his club in his hand.

"Oh, God!" exclaimed Nick and dropped me on the ground.

"Jeez!" said Peanuts softly.

I got up and ran to Ooma. "Thank you, Ooma, Leroy need help."

Peanuts and the others stood frozen in fear.

Ooma stepped toward them and raised his club. "Ooma fix so no hurt Leroy again!"

"No," I said. "Let me talk to them." I pulled up my pants, got my shoes on, and walked over to where they stood.

"You guys believe me now?"

"Yeah," said Peanuts, "we believe you."

I looked at Danny. "Am I a bullslinger?"

"No," he said shakily, "you're not."

"Not what?"

"You're not a bullslinger."

"You gonna mess with me again, Nick?"

"N-n-no!"

"Ooma is my friend," I said. "Everything I told you was true. Until the professor wakes up, this is a secret. You guys understand?"

"We ain't telling nobody," said Peanuts. "We promise. You can trust us. Just don't let him do nothing, okay?"

"Not if you keep quiet. But if anybody talks, you'll have to answer to Ooma. Got that?"

"We got it," said Danny.

"Then you guys get out of here and keep your mouths shut!"

"We'll leave," said Nick.

I turned to Ooma. "Let's go to your tree."

The Neanderthal took my hand, and together we started away.

Looking back over my shoulder, I called, "See you guys in school tomorrow!"

They looked at me but didn't reply.

I rubbed my hand over my pocket. The lucky penny was still there. It had worked after all.

If I only knew!

11

A BROKEN PROMISE

"I don't trust them," said Willie.

"Me either," said Melissa.

It was evening. We were sitting on Willie's front porch while Doc patrolled the block making sure that everyone's blackout curtains were pulled down.

"Well then," I said, "shall I tell my mom about Ooma tonight? She can call Chief West. We can explain things to him. Maybe he'll understand and be careful."

Willie scratched his head. "I hate to think of Ooma being kept in jail while some FBI agent shines a light in his face and asks him a bunch of questions he doesn't understand. Or even worse, he might get put in a hospital like I was. Then a bunch of strange doctors will start sticking needles in him."

"Boy," I said in frustration, "I sure messed things up when I told those guys the Neanderthal story."

"Don't worry about it," said Willie. "How could you know that they'd make you take them into the canyon?"

Melissa sighed. "They might tell everyone, and they might not say a thing."

"Then let's not jump to conclusions," said Willie. "Let's wait and see what Peanuts and the guys say tomorrow. I asked my mom about comas. She said that people can come out of them anytime."

"Or not at all," I added. "That's our problem."

"I vote for at least one more day," said Melissa. "See what they say at school tomorrow."

I looked at her. "Are you saying that because you want me to take you down there to see him?"

She shook her head. "I want to go, but I can't. Doc would be too upset if I didn't come straight home from school. No, I'd rather see the Neanderthal taken proper care of by the professor. Everybody else will be guessing what to do, and someone might hurt him."

"All right," I said, "then I'll wait and see what happens tomorrow."

The next day, I took my yo-yo to school. At morning recess, I stood on the grass with a bunch of guys practicing tricks.

Melissa showed up and motioned for me to come over to her.

"I've thought it over, and I've changed my mind," she said.

"About what?"

"I think you should tell your mother about the Neanderthal and get him out of the canyon as fast as possible. I don't trust those boys. Right now, they're sitting together down by the barbecue. I think they're going to do something bad to the Neanderthal."

Her turnabout caught me by surprise. "Boy, Melissa, get you! You're always talking about my imagination. Now who's carrying on?"

"I thought about it all last night and all this morning. Something bad is going to happen. I can just feel it when I look at them."

"Well, I thought it over too," I replied. "And I agree with what you and Willie said last night. The Neanderthal is used to the canyon, and he's safe there. I think we should wait another day or two and see if the professor comes out of his coma."

"But I'm just sure they're up to something!"

"They're probably talking about putting me in a trash can again. I don't think they'll try it, though. This time they're stuck, and they know it."

Melissa scowled. "They're not stuck, Leroy. Boys like that are never stuck. They always come up with something, even if it's stupid. I'm going to keep an eye on them."

I flipped my yo-yo out and to my surprise it shot straight back into my hand.

Melissa shook her head. "Really, Leroy! They're

going to do something to the Neanderthal, and you're playing with a yo-yo!"

She stalked off to the end of the field where she could watch the conversation at the barbecue.

I returned to the grass where I spent the rest of recess trying to repeat what I'd done by accident.

At lunch, Melissa came over to the bench where I was eating with the German Ace.

"Leroy," she said, "Peanuts is sitting alone down by the barbecue. I don't see the others around anywhere."

"Calm down, Melissa, they're probably in the bathroom. I promise, if they say anything to me, I'll tell my mom right away."

"But she works until late!"

"Look, Willie said not to jump to conclusions and I agree."

"All right for you!" she snapped, and turned quickly and walked away.

After she left, I couldn't concentrate on anything for very long. I tried fighter-plane tag, I tried my yo-yo, but all I really did was to look for Nick, Danny, and Marty. They were nowhere to be seen.

Finally, I began to think that Melissa was right. Something was going on all right, but what? As lunch ended, I went back to class feeling very uneasy.

The bell for afternoon recess rang, and I walked out the door and headed down the hallway.

"Leroy!"

I looked to my right and saw Peanuts next to me.

"Meet me in the rest room by room six in five minutes."

"Why?" I asked.

He turned and walked away without replying.

I went to the end of the corridor and out onto the yard. What was I going to do for five minutes? I took out my yo-yo, looked at it, and put it back in my pocket.

Melissa was not by the benches, rings, or hopscotch courts. I found her at the edge of the grass, still watching the barbecue area.

"You're right," I said. "Something is going on." Then I told her what happened with Peanuts.

She spoke excitedly. "I'll be by the benches. I'm not going back to class until you tell me what he said."

"Okay, meet you there."

As I neared the rest room, two boys came bursting out of the doors.

"Who does he think he is?" grumbled one. "He can't order us out."

"That's Peanuts McGruder," said the other. "You don't want to mess around with him. Let's go to the rest room by room twelve."

I pushed the door open and went in.

Peanuts was leaning against a washbowl with his arms folded across his chest. When I entered he straightened up and walked over to me.

"Leroy," he said, "I ain't a rat."

I stepped back. "I never said you were."

"That's not what I mean. Danny, Nick, and Marty have made up a story. I didn't have nothing to do with it. When I promise something, I mean it. I promised that I wasn't going to say nothing about the caveman. I haven't, but they have!"

"Who did they tell?"

"Their parents and the police."

"The police? Did they tell them everything?"

Before he could reply, the rest room door was pushed open and a short, curly-haired boy entered.

Peanuts raised his fist. "Private conversation. Get lost!"

The boy made a quick U-turn, stumbled over his own feet, and ran out the exit door.

Peanuts looked back at me. "I said they made up a story. They wanted me to go in with them, but I told them I wasn't having anything to do with it."

"But why would they make up a story?"

"Because they don't want it to seem like anything was their fault. They're mad at you. They want to get the caveman captured, and they want the credit for it. That's why."

"What did they say?"

"They said that a crazy man living in the canyon came up on the rim and called for help. They said he was dressed in rags and looked like a caveman. They said that when they went to help him, he picked up a club and chased them. They said he tried to kill them."

"Then the police will think that he's dangerous and go after him with guns. He could get shot!"

Peanuts stuffed his hands in his pockets. "You got it, pal! That's why I ain't having any part of it. I'm like you said I was in the story you told. I'm not a coward, and I'm not a rat. I'm telling you so that something can be done about it."

"But what?"

"Their mothers called the police this morning. The police chief himself was here at noon today talking to them. They're supposed to show where they went down in the canyon after school today."

"Then I've got to get the Neanderthal out of the canyon before they get to him."

Peanuts's expression suddenly changed. His mouth tightened, and his eyes narrowed. In one quick move he straightened up, took his hands from his pockets, and took a step toward me.

I jumped back. "Wait a minute, Peanuts. What did I say?"

His index finger shot out and stabbed me in the center of the chest.

"What makes you think you're going down there alone, Leroy?"

"I'm not?"

"No way, pal. I want to see this caveman close up again."

"You want to help me?" I said in amazement.

"Let's just say we're gonna rescue this caveman together, huh?"

"Sure," I said. "Sure!"

He nodded. "That's it then."

"Right," I said. "Meet you at the gate by the tennis courts right after school. Melissa will be with me."

He stopped. "A girl?"

I talked fast, not quite sure of where I was going. "She's the one who helped me figure out how to make contact with the caveman. She's an orphan, and she's tough. She's like those women in the movies who fight with the French underground against the Germans."

"An orphan in the French underground, huh?" said Peanuts. "I like that. Okay, she can help us!"

Peanuts had got things a little mixed up, but I was not about to correct him.

He pointed toward the doors. "You go out first, and I'll come out in a minute. I don't want those guys to see us together."

I left the rest room, headed straight to the benches, and told Melissa what was going on.

Her eyes narrowed. "What about Peanuts? Do you really think that we can trust him?"

"If he acts like he did in my story, we can."

"How will we get Ooma out of the canyon?"

"We'll dress him in my dad's old hat and coat. We'll head out the front of the canyon to the beach road. Then we'll take him to my house. I'll tell my mom what's going on and she can call Chief West."

The bell ending recess rang.

"See you after school," I said.

She hesitated. "I am going with you, aren't I? I mean forget what I said yesterday about not worrying Doc. This is too important. I have to help on this. And . . . uh . . . you won't let Peanuts talk you out of taking me, will you?"

"You're in," I said. "Just like Jane in the Dawn Patrol."

She smiled. "Tune in after school, huh?"

"Right," I said. "Tune in after school for the exciting conclusion."

"We'll do it," she said.

"I hope so," I replied.

"See you."

"See you."

The rest of the school day passed in a jumble of nerves.

12

THREE STARTLED MEN

I was out of my classroom door before the final bell had stopped ringing. Peanuts and Melissa were right behind me when I reached the gate.

"Down a block and across the vacant lot," I said to Peanuts as we ran.

Cutting through the lot saved time and kept us out of the way of Doc's house.

I found my dad's raincoat and hat in his closet. I got a couple of empty shopping bags from the kitchen. I carried the bag with the hat. Peanuts took the one with the coat.

"Come on," said Peanuts, "let's get moving."

"Hold it," I said looking at Melissa.

"What's wrong?" she asked.

"You can't go in a dress. You'll get all cut up."

Her face clouded. "But you promised you wouldn't leave me!"

"We won't." I went to my closet and returned with a pair of jeans, a shirt, and an old pair of tennis shoes. "Go in the bathroom and put this stuff on."

"And hurry!" ordered Peanuts.

In no time at all, the door opened and Melissa stepped out. She was gripping the pants at the waist.

"Leroy, these pants won't stay up."

I dug an old belt out of my drawer, and she tried it on.

"How's that?"

"Good," she said. "How do I look?"

"Like an underground fighter," I said.

"Yeah," agreed Peanuts. "Now come on. We don't have any time to lose."

Melissa put her dress and shoes in my closet. I locked the house.

"Wait a second," I said. "I want to talk to Willie Owens. He lives right across the street."

"What?" hollered Peanuts.

"Tell him about Willie," I said to Melissa, and I ran across the street and banged on Willie's screen door. The front door was open, and I could see into the living room. "Willie!" I yelled. "It's Leroy, are you in there?" A second later, Willie came, propelling himself in his wheelchair.

"What's going on?" he asked.

"Where's your mom?"

"At the market. Why?"

"I've got to talk to you fast. Peanuts is on our side, but the other guys told the police about the Neanderthal. They made up lies to make him sound dangerous. He could get shot. We're on our way to get him out!"

"Come on, Leroy!" came Peanuts's voice. I turned and saw him running across the street. Melissa was behind him.

"I gotta go, Willie." I turned and started down the steps.

"Leroy, wait. Don't go without me!"

"Look," cried Peanuts. "He's up!"

I turned and saw Willie standing on his feet, bracing himself against the screen door.

"Come on!" I urged.

The screen door opened. Willie, gripping the side of the door tightly, stepped out onto the porch.

"You can do it!" exclaimed Melissa.

Willie smiled but shook his head. "I want to, but I can't. My legs are too shaky. But I can stand, and I can walk a little. I didn't believe I could. Leroy, you've got the lucky penny. You guys save the Neanderthal. You've got to! And hurry!"

"He's right," said Peanuts. "We've got to get going!"

"See you later, Willie!" I called and turned toward Peanuts and Melissa. The three of us ran across the street and headed for the canyon.

* * *

When we arrived, we saw three police cars parked at the curb. The police and a group of people stood in the field.

"Look," said Melissa. "There's Danny, Nick, and Marty!"

"Yes," I replied. "They're talking to Chief West."

"There's the guy who chased us away from the canyon," said Peanuts.

"I'll bet that those other people live around here too," I said. "They saw the police and got curious."

We had taken a route that brought us to the canyon two blocks west of our usual spot. We had crossed onto the field and slowly made our way, from tree to tree, to where we were now. We were close enough to recognize people, but not close enough to hear what was being said. Above all, we did not want to be seen by Nick, Danny, or Marty.

"It doesn't look like they've gone down in the canyon yet," said Melissa.

"I wonder what they're waiting for?" I asked.

The answer arrived in the form of a large army truck that pulled around the corner and stopped at the curb.

An officer stepped from the passenger's side of the truck and walked over to Chief West. The two men spoke for a minute, then the officer signaled the driver who got out and walked to the back of the truck.

"All right, men, everybody out!" he hollered.

In a minute, two lines of soldiers in helmets and carrying rifles presented themselves to the group of police and onlookers.

The officer and the chief began talking to the soldiers.

"What's the army doing here?" I asked.

"I'll tell you," said Peanuts. "It says Fort McArthur on the side of that truck. I got an uncle stationed down there. Lots of soldiers are being trained and moved around now. Sometimes, when they get through doing one thing, it takes a couple of weeks for new orders to come in. These guys are probably waiting around and got nothing to do, so the chief is using them to check out the canyon. It'll be just like a training mission for them."

"Then we've got to get moving," I said. "If we stay here and watch them, we lose our head start."

"Where do we go down?" asked Melissa.

"We don't have time to be picky," I replied. "Let's make a run for the nearest spot."

Melissa grabbed my arm. "Leroy, I'm scared!"

"We got no time for being scared," said Peanuts.

I reached into my pocket. "Here, take this," I said. "It's Willie's lucky penny. Put it in your back pocket. Everything will be fine."

She did, and managed a slight smile.

I crouched down and looked at Peanuts. "Ready . . . set . . . go!"

We dashed to the edge and jumped over. Just

as we did, we heard someone yell, "Hey, you, stop!"

"Did you hear that?" asked Peanuts. "Was he yelling at us?"

"Probably," I said as I was grabbing at a limb and trying to keep my footing. "But we can't wait to find out now!"

We came to a large bush.

"Just like your story," said Peanuts, "commandos in the jungle!" He reached out and started snapping away some branches so we could get through.

Peanuts got down first and looked around. "Cripes!" He pointed up the canyon wall to the east. "Here comes the army!"

We could see the figures of the soldiers starting to descend. At the same time, someone was running along the canyon rim in our direction.

"Hey, you down there!" he called.

"Come on!" I said and we ran for the protection of the trees.

"They've definitely seen us," said Melissa as we pushed our way between some bushes and trees. "What do you think they'll do?"

"I don't know," I replied, "maybe they'll be a little more careful before they shoot and maybe not. Ooma is pretty scary when you first see him. No matter what happens, we've got to get to him before they do."

We could hear the shouts of the soldiers as they spread out across the canyon floor.

"Stop a minute," I said.

"What's wrong?" asked Peanuts.

"We're coming from a slightly different direction, and I'm a little lost."

"Come on," urged Peanuts, "what direction do you think it's in? Once those soldiers spread out, they'll start moving toward us."

I tried to see the canyon rim so I could get my bearings, but our view was blocked all around by the trees.

The voices of the soldiers continued to fill the air.

"Hurry, Leroy!" said Melissa.

I pointed. "That way, I think."

"Then let's go."

Ten minutes later, we came out from under a grove of trees and stopped.

"There's his tree!" I exclaimed, pointing to the willow. "Ooma!" I shouted. "Ooma, Leroy here!"

"Quiet!" hissed Peanuts. "You'll give our position away."

Ooma's deep voice filled the air. *"Friend, Leroy, Ooma here."* He stepped out from the tree holding his club in one hand and the white skull in the other.

"Oh-my-gosh," Melissa whispered, "he *is* real!"

I grabbed her arm and walked her up to him. Peanuts followed. I pointed to each of them. "This friend Melissa and friend Peanuts. They help Ooma and Leroy now."

Ooma looked around. "Many voices in air. Many people come. Professor say many people come see Ooma."

"No," I said. "Not these people. We have to get away from these people. We have to go now. We're going out toward the ocean." I pointed in what I thought was the right direction. "That way. Do you understand, Ooma?"

He nodded. "Ooma know way to ocean." He held out the white skull to Melissa. "Melissa take skull of cave bear. Bring luck. Ooma need two hands."

"And I thought it was a big dog!" said Peanuts.

"Thank you," said Melissa trying to be polite, but she couldn't hide a grimace as she took the skull.

The soldiers' voices continued to grow louder.

Peanuts grabbed my arm. "They're close. Get moving. I'll bring up the rear. If I see them, I'll make a lot of noise and lead them in the wrong direction."

"You can bring up the rear," I said, "but stay with us. We don't want to lose you." I turned to Ooma. "Let's go."

Following Ooma was like being behind a human bulldozer. One massive hand would crack branches while the other, swinging his club, made an opening through bushes and undergrowth.

The voices of the soldiers continued to pursue us. "You doing all right, Melissa?" I asked.

"Of course," she panted, "I've got the lucky penny and the lucky bear skull. How are you doing?"

"Fine, I just wish we were out of here."

I looked back at Peanuts and saw that he was continually checking behind us.

He looked at me. "We're still ahead of them."

"You want to switch the hat and coat?" I asked. "The hat's a lot lighter."

"No, it's okay, just keep moving."

We did. Ducking under branches, climbing over fallen trees, getting scratched, getting rocks in our shoes, stumbling, picking ourselves up, we kept moving toward the ocean.

"Hold it," said Peanuts. "I want to check on the soldiers."

He ran back down a small hill, listened, and called, "I hear them, they're coming all right."

I looked around. "We've been going a long time," I said to Melissa. "We must be fairly close to the ocean."

"Men up ahead," said Ooma.

I stopped. "What men? How do you know?"

"Ooma come here twice before. Once see three men. Next time men gone, but place where men stay still here."

"Did you talk to them?"

He shook his head. "Men speak strange. Ooma not understand. Stay hidden."

"Let's go look," I said to him. "Peanuts, stay with Melissa. We'll be right back."

"Be careful," he said.

"I will. Maybe they're just some drifters."

There was a narrow space between some trees that resembled a path. It ended at a bunch of bushes. I started along the path ahead of Ooma. I found myself going slightly downhill and picked up some speed. Suddenly I felt good and began to trot. I cut around the bushes and ducked under the drooping limb of a large tree.

"Leroy!" came Ooma's voice from behind me.

"What?" I said, but I didn't stop. I pushed through leafy limbs that were hanging to the ground, rounded another bush, and found myself staring at three startled men, a small tent, some suitcases, and a black radio with an antenna.

"Excuse me!" I said and started to turn back.

"Hold it, kid!" said one of the men.

"No, I've got to leave."

"No you don't. Hold it right there." The man stood up. There was a large, silver pistol in his hand, and it pointed straight at me!

13

THE FIGHT

"I know you," I blurted out. "You're the German saboteurs! Your pictures were in the newspaper."

Heinz Muller grabbed me. "Too bad for you," he said coldly.

"You better let go of me. The United States Army is on its way here right now."

Werner Bauer gave a sad smile. "Those things only happen in American cowboy movies. Unfortunately for you, this is a real war, and we're going to have to kill you."

"Ooma!" I cried.

Ernst Wald looked puzzled. "Ooma?"

"*Le-roy*!" boomed the Neanderthal's voice as he came crashing through the bushes waving his club over his head.

Heinz Muller gasped, *"Mein Gott!"* He stepped behind me and held me tightly.

Werner Bauer whirled around, caught sight of Ooma, and froze. That was his mistake. Ooma let go of his club like it was a boomerang. It flew end over end and caught the German full across the chest.

"Ach!" he cried as he fell over backward. His gun fired harmlessly into the air and dropped from his hand to the ground.

Ernst Wald made a quick move toward it.

"Get him, Ooma," I yelled.

The Nazi's eyes widened, and he stopped in his tracks. *"Himmel!"* he gasped.

Ooma reached down. With a grunt, he lifted Ernst Wald over his head. Then he looked at Heinz Muller. "Let boy go or Ooma break man in half!"

I heard Muller gasp behind me.

Wald, suspended in the air, cried, "Heinz, do what he says!"

Muller bellowed, "You think I'm a fool? The boy is my protection!" Holding me tightly with his left arm, he reached his right hand down and came up with a small revolver which had been strapped to his lower leg.

"Eee-Yahh!" came a scream from the bushes, and the paper bag containing the raincoat came sailing through the air in our direction.

Startled, Muller fired at the bag, and I did the only

thing I could think of. I stomped down on his foot as hard as I could.

"Ahhh!" he yelled.

I twisted hard, got part way out of his grasp, and fell on the ground.

"Swine!" Muller snarled, and I saw the gun moving my way.

"No hurt boy!" came Ooma's deep voice.

"I'll kill you!" cried Muller quickly raising the gun.

Ooma gave a fearsome growl. Then he lunged forward and hurled Ernst Wald, like a sack of potatoes, right at Heinz Muller.

Muller's gun fired once. I saw Ooma throw his hands over his face and fall forward. Then the two Nazis collided and crashed to the ground in a heap.

For a moment, everything was very quiet.

I lay flat on the ground with my face buried in my arms. I was afraid to look up, afraid that Ooma was dead!

A hand grabbed at me. I heard groans.

"Leroy, are you all right?" asked Melissa.

"Hey," said Peanuts, "can you talk? Who are these guys?"

"I'm all right," I answered as they helped me up. I opened my eyes and looked about me. "They're the Nazis whose pictures were in the paper."

Heinz Muller and Ernst Wald were lying next to each other. Both were clutching their ribs and moaning.

Werner Bauer still lay on his back where he had fallen. He seemed to be unconscious.

Ooma, himself, lay flat on the ground. Melissa ran over and knelt next to him.

"Ooma, get up!" she pleaded. "Please, get up!"

There was no response.

She reached out her hand and placed it on Ooma's shoulder.

Slowly, the Neanderthal's head lifted, and he pushed himself up to a sitting position. There was blood on the right side of his face.

"Ooma!" I cried, and ran over to him.

The blood came from a gash that was just above his right eyebrow.

"The bullet must have grazed him," said Peanuts. "He'll be okay."

There was a dazed look on Ooma's face.

"Ooma," I said, "do you know who I am?"

He looked at me but did not reply.

Suddenly, Melissa screamed, "Leroy, that Nazi has a gun!"

I looked to my right and saw that Werner Bauer had rolled over and reached the gun that had fallen from his hand. He grabbed it and started slowly rising.

"Do something!" Melissa pleaded.

I looked helplessly at Peanuts, and he returned my look.

"Here!" Melissa cried. She bent quickly, picked

up Heinz Muller's pistol, and shoved it into my hand. "Shoot him, Leroy!"

Bauer was standing, but not well. He was hunched forward, his left hand clutching his chest where the club had hit him. His right hand, holding the large pistol, hung down at his side. The barrel pointed at the ground.

On his face was an expression of hate and pain. His lips were parted and his teeth were clenched. Then, very slowly, he started to move toward us.

I took, I believe, two or three steps in his direction, lifted my trembling hand, and pointed the gun.

"Do it, Leroy," urged Peanuts. "Shoot him!"

My hand shook so much, the gun seemed to dance in it.

Werner Bauer stopped, started to raise his gun, and then began to cough. He panted and coughed more. He wiped his left hand across his mouth, and it came away with blood on it. "You'll all die!" he gasped. But the coughing came again and shook his whole body.

It looked like he tried to take another step toward us but couldn't. His body stiffened, and when it did, the gun went off. The bullet struck the ground a few feet in front of him. His lips moved soundlessly, his knees buckled, and he toppled forward into the dirt. The gun landed about two feet from his body.

I dropped my arm and sighed with relief.

"I'm getting that gun!" said Peanuts.

"No!" begged Melissa.

But Peanuts was gone. He dashed over to where Bauer lay, scooped up the gun, and ran back without stopping.

That's when Ooma, the dazed look gone from his face, stared at us and said in perfect English, "My God! What's been going on around here?"

Before we could react, a voice from our left hollered, "All right down there, everybody freeze!"

We looked up to find ourselves surrounded by soldiers with rifles pointed at us. An officer with a pistol in his hand pointed at us and commanded, "You two boys, set those guns on the ground!"

We did.

The officer then began to walk toward us. As we watched, Chief West and an older-looking man dressed in street clothes hurriedly joined him.

Ooma stood up and turned around. I immediately jumped in front of him.

"Don't shoot him, Chief! He's not like a bull in a china shop." I pointed to the Germans. "These men are the Nazi saboteurs whose pictures were in the paper. The Neanderthal just captured them. That's what the gunshots were all about. Please, don't shoot him!"

"Don't worry, Leroy," said the chief as he walked up to us. "I wasn't serious. I never imagined anything like this happening."

Then he looked at the Germans. "It's them, all

right," he said to the officer. "It looks like we got more than we bargained for today."

The officer motioned to the soldiers, and several of them ran over. They tied the Germans' hands behind their backs and began searching them.

One of the soldiers opened a suitcase and exclaimed, "Hey, this thing is full of incendiary bombs! And here are maps of the city and Douglas Aircraft."

The old man moved quickly over to Ooma. "Ottis," he said, "are you all right?"

Ooma looked at the old man. "Professor Ludlow," he said "am I glad to see you. What happened?"

"We had an accident. I lost control of the car. Don't you remember?"

Ooma put his hand to his head, and his eyes seemed to look inward. "Yes . . . yes I do remember! We had just finished working the carnival in Santa Barbara. We were headed for the sideshow at the pier in Long Beach. We were on a tight schedule, so I didn't change out of my costume."

"Your costume?" said Melissa.

"Yes," said Ooma. "This is a costume."

"We thought you were a Neanderthal man," said Peanuts.

"He is!" said the professor. "At carnivals and sideshows. That's our act. We're known as 'Professor Ludlow and the Neanderthal Man.' I explain to the audience how, one day, I was working on an electrical experiment when something unexpected happened.

I was somehow able to reach into the past and bring back a Neanderthal man. I demonstrate my electrical machine, which throws a lot of wonderful-looking sparks. Then Ottis, here, comes on. He tells what it was like to live in prehistoric times. We let the audience ask him questions. He's memorized everything science knows about prehistoric life. Nobody ever trips him up!"

I looked up at Ooma. "Your name is Ottis?"

"Yes," he replied. "I'm Ottis Beers. I'm from Bakersfield, California. I used to work on a farm, until I met the professor. His last partner had quit, and he needed a new one. He said that if I'd grow a beard, I'd be the best-looking Neanderthal he'd ever had."

"You sure fooled us," Peanuts said.

Mr. Beers shook his head. "I didn't try to fool you. There was the accident and then . . . this is the first time I can remember anything but . . . but our act. I thought I was Ooma until that bullet grazed my head." He pointed to the Germans. "Only a Neanderthal would have taken on three men with guns!"

"Whether you meant to or not," said the chief, "all four of you are heroes."

"Will we get our pictures in the papers?" asked Peanuts.

"I can't promise you that," said the chief. "But you certainly will receive some kind of recognition."

Professor Ludlow took Mr. Beers aside and they began talking about what had happened.

The chief looked steadily at us. "I don't suppose that any of your folks has the slightest idea that you were planning to trespass into this canyon today, do they?"

We looked at each other. "Oh no!" we chorused. "Our folks—"

14

THE LUCKY PENNY

If you ever need someone to get you out of trouble, the chief of police isn't a bad person to pick. I mean, what could anyone say when he drove us home in his car and explained that we were heroes?

At seven that evening, we all met at the police station. This time though, my mother, Doc, and Peanuts's parents were with us.

We gave statements to the FBI men, who were all dressed in gray suits and looked pretty much alike.

After that, FBI agents Richardson and Grenville spoke to us.

Agent Grenville held up a blue work suit with the

lettering L.A. COUNTY GAS COMPANY on the front and back.

"These are not real uniforms, but most people don't know the difference. The Germans have been using them to get into houses and businesses around Douglas Aircraft. When they crawl under a building to make an inspection, they plant an incendiary bomb with a timing device on it. The devices are set to go off at midnight tonight. With the entire city blacked out, you can imagine how clearly Douglas would be outlined.

"A Japanese submarine with a catapult plane on its deck is set to surface when the incendiaries go off. The plane would fly in quickly and drop its bombs on the aircraft plant.

"Our men are now disarming the bombs, and our navy is ready for the sub."

Agent Richardson said firmly, "We're going to clamp the War Secrecy Act on this whole affair. That means as far as the public is concerned, none of this ever happened. There will be no reports in the papers, and you will not be able to talk about this to anyone. It's in America's best interest that the enemy not know how close they came, and that people not be made more fearful of attack."

"You mean no pictures in the paper?" said Peanuts.

"I'm afraid not. However, you do deserve something more than a pat on the back and a certificate at the end of the war. Let's think it over and maybe we can come up with something, all right?"

We agreed, the meeting ended, and everyone went home.

The FBI was true to their word. We did get more than a pat on the back. Donald Douglas himself led us on a tour of his aircraft plant. And Willie got to go with us.

The highlight of our visit was having our picture taken standing by the giant tire of the B-19.

Nick, Danny, and Marty never did find out what happened down in the canyon. Danny tried once. He approached Peanuts during morning recess.

"Hey, Peanuts," he said. "You can tell me. What happened that day in the canyon?"

"I don't know what you're talking about," replied Peanuts. "And keep away from my friends or you'll be chewing on your own teeth, get me?"

Danny got him, and so did Nick and Marty.

"Know what?" Willie said to me one day as we walked slowly around the block together.

"What?" I replied as I leaned over and yanked a weed out of a vacant lot.

"It could have happened for real."

"What are you talking about?"

"That Neanderthal business. It could have been a real time machine."

I stuck the thin weed in the space between my two front teeth. "But it wasn't a real time machine."

"I know it wasn't," he protested, "but it could have been. I mean, somebody could invent a time machine and bring a real Neanderthal man into today. Maybe someday it will actually happen! There's this article in the latest edition of—"

"Look, Willie," I said cutting him off, "when I told you about him, what did you think he was?"

"A Neanderthal man."

"Right," I said. "He was real to you, and he was real to me. We all believed it. So it doesn't matter to me what happens in the future because for four days I knew a real Neanderthal man. Not many people can say that."

Willie smiled. "No," he said looking down at his legs, "you're right. Not many people can."

He dug his hand deeply into his pocket, pulled out his lucky penny, and flipped it high into the air.